THE GOALIE WHO STOLE CHRISTMAS

A HOLIDAY NOVELLA

WYNCOTE WOLVES
BOOK FIVE

CALI MELLE

- To all the holiday lovin' babes -
May your holiday's be sweet and spicy.

PROLOGUE
ASHER

Of course, this is the exact situation I should have expected to find myself in. Even though I'm the middle child, I always expected that I would be the last one of my siblings to get married. I never quite fit in with the way they live their lives and I've always been a little different than the rest of them. My mother always seemed to be accepting of it, but over the past few years, she's really put on the pressure for me to settle down with someone.

I know she knows how important hockey is and how it will always come first. I also know that after her breast cancer diagnosis last year, she has wanted to speed up everything in her children's lives. I'm sure there's a weird sense of being reminded of her mortality.

Thankfully, she was able to have a double mastectomy and undergo chemotherapy in an effort to stop any other possible cancer cells in her body. The doctors are hoping that she is in remission, but there's a part of her that doesn't think she's going to make it out alive. And that has been the reason why she's pushing so hard for everyone to speed things up in their lives.

Even though she's only in her fifties, she's terrified she won't see all of her children get married. She won't get to see her grandchildren. My mother knows how I am; she knows I don't seriously date anyone. I may have in high school, but that didn't really count. Now, she's been pushing so hard and constantly questioning me on why I'm still single.

I've tried to ignore her, but she just won't let it go. Literally over the past year, since she was diagnosed, my two older sisters got married and now my little brother is getting married later this month. Which leaves me as the one who gets to be the disappointment. The one kid who doesn't have anyone, who would rather be alone and just focus on the life that I'm trying to build around hockey.

My parents were supportive—they still are—but

my mother wants me to experience other things in life. Even though by going to the professional league I will be set for the rest of my life, none of that matters. And that's easy for her to say. She and my father have already built a life together, so she doesn't have to worry about how she will pay the bills or take care of herself.

And there's a part of her that doesn't want me to worry about those things either, but I'm not going to rely on my parents. Not at twenty-one years old. I haven't lived with them in almost three years, I'm not going back to that life now.

I barely even pay attention during any of my classes today, because my brain is so focused on the messages my mother sent me this morning. She's asking if I'm bringing a plus-one to the wedding. And the truth is, no... I don't have a date. I didn't have any plans to find one, but now the pressure is on.

The last thing I want to do is disappoint my mother.

So, it looks like I'm finding a fake girlfriend to take to my brother's wedding.

CHAPTER ONE
ASHER

"I need your help," I tell Cameron, my voice low as we follow the rest of the team after our practice. Cam stops short, turning around to face me just outside of the locker room.

"What's up, Ash?" he asks, tilting his head to the side as he runs a hand through his sweaty hair. "Is everything okay?"

I shrug, clutching my helmet between my torso and my arm. "I need your help to find a girl. I need a date to my brother's wedding."

Cam raises an eyebrow. "Your entire family knows that you're single, so why do you need to take someone? And isn't the wedding at the end of the month?"

I nod, shifting my weight on my skates. "My

mom has been freaking out with her cancer scare and everything. She won't leave me alone about being single, so I would rather just show up there with someone and get her off my back. That way she can enjoy my brother's wedding and shit. I literally just need to find someone who will pretend to be my girlfriend, travel to Maine for the weekend with me, and then we can go our separate ways."

"And you seem to think that I might know of someone?"

"I don't know. I'm at a complete loss here, so I just need help finding someone. Anyone, literally."

"Have you talked to any of the other guys? You know, most people are going home for the holidays. It might be hard to find a date to go with you, with Christmas being so close."

A sigh slips from my lips and we both begin to walk into the locker room. Cam is right and it wasn't something I had really thought about. I don't know why Andrew and Evelyn had to pick four days before Christmas to get married, but that's what they did.

There has to be someone who doesn't feel like going home for the holidays. Or someone who would rather get a free trip for Christmas instead.

Cameron doesn't say anything to the other guys

as we all begin taking off our gear in the locker room, although I don't miss the way he keeps glancing at me expectantly. I'm not sure how to bring it up to them, but if there's anyone who can help me find a date, it's definitely one of the guys in here.

"Guys, I need all of your help," I announce, my voice louder than the sounds of their laughter and conversation as everyone finishes getting changed. They all stand up, their attention directed at me. "I need to find a date to take to my brother's wedding in two weeks."

Logan and August break from their conversation, looking at me from where they're seated. Cam has a huge grin on his face and he nods at me in approval. I know he was probably wondering when I was going to say something and it was probably killing him to not say anything. I glance around the rest of the room, my eyes going past Sterling and Simon, before landing on Hayden who leans against his locker with a smirk on his face.

"Where's the wedding?" Simon asks, his voice curious from where he's sitting. "And what's the deal with the date?"

"It's in my hometown in Maine. I need to find someone who will pretend to be my girlfriend and be my date, to appease my mom. After we get back, we can go back to how things were before."

Hayden starts to walk toward me. "Do you have any girls in mind? You know with Christmas, it might be hard to find someone."

Tilting my head to the side, I narrow my gaze on his. "Tell me, King," I start to question him. "Do you plan on going home for the holidays?"

His jaw clenches and he doesn't say a single word as he collects his things and leaves the room. It was fucked up of me to come at him with a low blow, but I already know the position I'm in right now. And Hayden doesn't get to say a damn thing. The only reason he's here is because he fucked up at the last university he was at. I know some of the guys know him from childhood and don't get me wrong, Hayden King is a good guy, but he needs to check himself sometimes.

"That was a low blow, man," Cam says, shaking his head at me. "You know that's a touchy subject for Hayden."

Swallowing roughly, I hang my head in defeat. I'm frustrated from the entire situation I've gotten myself in and Cam's right. I owe Hayden an apology. That wasn't fair to him, but shit. I already know how hard this is going to be to find someone to agree, not to mention how difficult it will be with Christmas so soon.

"So, you don't have anyone in mind, do you?" Simon questions me again. "All right, boys," he says to the rest of the guys. "We got some work to do. Find whatever girls you know would be down for a good time with our man here."

They all begin to hoot and holler, like they actually give a shit about it, before everyone goes their separate ways for the night. Shaking my head, I pull out my phone and send Hayden a message to apologize before getting the rest of my stuff together. I head out of the locker room, leaving the guys to themselves as they develop a plan.

It's Operation Find Asher A Date.

Who knows how the hell this is going to go...

———

"Hey, Ash," Sydney's voice floats through my ears as she walks up to me and takes a seat next to me. I glance over at her, her bright blue eyes shining at me as she flashes her perfect white teeth. My eyes trail over her face, free of any makeup. Her bright blonde hair is pulled up into a messy bun on the top of her head and I smile at her carefree appearance. "How was your weekend?"

I've known Sydney since freshman year. We met that year in some of our classes and we've been friends since then. Somehow, we ended up having the same major, so that ended up with us having a lot of classes together. Sydney has always been like a breath of fresh air, a friend that I look forward to seeing each day. She makes my classes a little more tolerable.

"Meh." I shrug, offering her a small smile. "You know, same shit, different day."

"Heard that," she concurs as she unpacks her bag and slaps her notebook onto her desk. "I'm ready for this week to be over so we can finally have our winter break. Do you have any plans for our time off? Are you going home or anything?"

I nod. "I have to go back to Maine for my brother's wedding and then I'm going to be staying for Christmas before coming back home. What about you? Are you going back to California for the break?"

Sydney barks out a laugh and rolls her eyes as she shakes her head. "Absolutely not. My parents are traveling for the holiday, so there's no point in me going back there just to be alone."

I stare at my friend for a moment as she drops

her gaze down to the book in front of her. When I was trying to think of anyone who could be my fake girlfriend, Sydney didn't even cross my mind until now. She would be perfect. We already have a great friendship and get along easily, I don't think it would be a hard sell to my mother. And Sydney is going to be alone for the holidays, so it's actually quite perfect.

"I have a proposition for you," I offer, my voice quiet as Sydney lifts her blue eyes to mine. She's full of nothing but curiosity as her gaze bounces back and forth between my eyes. "Would you want to go to Maine with me for Christmas?"

Sydney tilts her head to the side, her eyebrows drawn together. "You mean, to stay with your family?"

Swallowing hard over my anxiety, I nod. "So, my brother is getting married four days before Christmas. I'm supposed to be his best man and my mom is expecting me to bring a date with me. You wouldn't have to stay for Christmas if you didn't want to, but the offer is open if you want."

"What's the catch?" Sydney questions me with a look of curiosity mixed with mischief.

"You have to pretend to be my girlfriend."

CHAPTER TWO
SYDNEY

I stare back at Asher, a little thrown off by his proposition, but I would be lying if I said I wasn't a little bit intrigued.

"That's it?" I ask him as he blinks at me like he's in shock. It's almost as if he didn't think I would agree to it without wanting some kinds of strings attached.

I've known Asher for three years and that's enough time to figure a person out. I love the guy and he's one of my closest friends, but I also know how he is. Asher doesn't do attachments and he doesn't do relationships. I would be a fool to ever have some unrealistic expectations like that of him.

"You mean you're considering it?" he asks, his

voice hopeful as his eyes widen slightly. "I just need you to come to the wedding with me and play the part so my mom is happy and then when we get back here, we can go back to the way things were before."

My heart sinks a little at his open admission. I've spent the past three years being Asher's friend, even though there was a small part of me that had always hoped for something more with him. He's a great guy, but I've learned that a relationship is something he isn't capable of. I can do this for him, even though it might mess with my mind and heart in the process.

"Do you want me to stay for Christmas too?"

Asher's smile widens and he suddenly appears shy as he nods and shrugs. "It would make things a little easier, but I don't expect that from you. But if you want to stay, I would love having you. It would help keep everyone off my back."

"Why are they so persistent you not to be single?" I ask him while I organize my papers in front of me just as our professor strolls into the room. "Don't they know by now that you're already tied down to a sport that is more demanding than any woman?"

Asher chuckles. "They know that, but my mom has big plans for all of her children. Ever since she was diagnosed with cancer last year, she's been persistent that we all get married ASAP and start popping out kids."

My eyes widen and I stare back at him. "And you're asking me to be your pretend girlfriend, taking me into a war zone like that?"

Asher laughs again, shaking his head. "She'll leave you alone about that. She'll just be surprised and thrilled enough to see that I'm not going to another wedding stag."

"Fine, fine," I throw my hands up in defeat, laughing along with my friend, "I'll go with you and I'll stay for the holiday. But I need you to promise me something..."

He tilts his head to the side. "If you're agreeing to save me, I owe you everything. So, I will promise you whatever you need."

"Promise me you won't fall in love with me," I tell him, my voice soft and serious as I stare back at him. Asher falls still for a moment, an eyebrow pulling upward. "After the holiday, we go back to being friends."

"That won't be a problem, Syd," he offers, a

smile forming on his lips. "I don't fall in love, so that's not even an option."

"Good," I tell him, nodding as I attempt to convince myself that Asher is a man of his word. "Because the last thing I need is our friendship getting ruined because of this little arrangement."

Asher offers his hand to me, shaking it after I slide my palm against his. "You have yourself a deal, Sydney Phillips. I promise I won't fall in love with you, as long as you pretend to be my fake girlfriend."

I smile back at him, shaking his hand as the warmth of his skin sends a shiver down my spine. "Deal."

Our professor begins to start our lecture for the day and Asher pulls his hand away from mine, directing his attention to the front of the class. I try to focus on my classwork, but it's practically impossible as my mind keeps floating back to Asher's proposition. It's actually quite enticing and it's not like I have anything else going on to keep me occupied.

To be honest, my plans for Christmas break involved binge-watching a lot of shows on Netflix that I haven't caught up on yet. I know, I know, it sounds pretty damn exhilarating. My parents did invite me to go traveling with them, but since I graduated from high school, it's become their new thing. And for once, I just wanted to have a normal holiday.

So, I guess I'm going to be normal by going to my fake boyfriend's brother's wedding and spending the holiday with his family.

This isn't going to be awkward at all.

All I have to do is play the part and make it as believable as I can. When I made Asher promise that he wouldn't fall in love with me, it was partially a joke, but there was also a seriousness behind my words too. The last thing we need is for either of us to go and develop some kind of feelings for the other and complicate everything.

I've already been hiding my own feelings for him and forcing myself to keep our friendship as it has always been. I don't want to ruin what we have, and I know Asher could never give me what I need. Which is exactly why I've chosen to ignore those feelings to preserve what we already have. The last thing I need is for him to be the one to develop feelings and not be able to ignore them.

Because our friendship would never survive a blow like that.

Before I realize it, class is over and the other students are already filing out of the room. Asher rises to his feet, rounding the desk as he watches me for a moment. "You all right, Syd?"

My eyes snap to his and I nod, forcing a smile on my face as I shove my things into my bag and rise to my feet. "Yep. I was just zoning out a little bit."

Asher watches me for a moment, his lips parting before he clamps them shut and he just nods instead. I'm not sure what words were lingering on the tip of his tongue, but I would love to hear them. Anything that could help calm my nerves right now, because I'm about to start second-guessing myself and this situation that I've gotten myself in.

"I'll see you later this afternoon?" he offers as the two of us walk out into the hallway, both turning to go in opposite directions. "Since break starts after the end of this week, maybe we can get together one of these days to the discuss specifics of the trip?"

I swallow nervously. "Sounds perfect!" I throw back to him, my voice sounding completely off. Asher's eyebrows pull together for a moment before he recovers and waves.

I watch him as he disappears down the hallway and I'm ready for the ground to open up and swallow me whole. *Get it together, Sydney. Asher is still your friend and this changes nothing.*

If I can convince myself of that, that would be great.

Because this is going to be the longest holiday break of my life.

CHAPTER THREE
ASHER

"So, I think I might have a girl who would agree to the whole situation," Cameron offers as he skates over to me during our warm-up. I'm currently in an almost split-like position on the ice, stretching out my legs before the guys start shooting at me.

I look up at Cam as I continue stretching. "I already took care of it and found someone."

Cam tilts his head to the side, his eyes finding mine through the cage of his helmet. "Who?"

"Sydney."

"Sydney Phillips?" Simon questions as he skates up to the two of us. "Shit. Are you sure you want her to just be your fake girlfriend? Because she's quite the catch."

"Yeah, but Sydney doesn't date," Sterling interjects as he shows up too. I glance behind him, noticing Hayden as he skates over with Logan and August. "Did you guys hear? Ash got Sydney to agree to be his fake date."

"No shit," August chuckles, shaking his head.

"Who's Sydney?" Hayden asks and for a moment, I feel kind of bad. Too often, we all seem to forget that he's still new here and doesn't know anyone really, except for the team.

"Asher's been friends with her since freshman year," Cam explains to him, shrugging before wagging his eyebrows at me. "Although, with how close the two of them are, I find it hard to believe that Ash would really keep a girl like her in the friend zone."

"Shut up," I mumble, stretching my legs a different way as my skates slide through the ice. "Sydney has always been a friend and I'm not going to fuck that up. I'm just glad she agreed to do this for me, because I already know that I can stand her presence."

The guys start laughing, all of them giving me shit about Syd like there's something they know that I don't. They're not wrong—she's definitely a catch and anyone would be lucky as hell to have her. But I can't look at her like that. Sydney and I are too good of friends to go and ruin that.

"She agreed to pretend to be your girlfriend? Is she going to stay with your family for Christmas too?"

"Yep." I smile at the guys, nodding as I practice my different stances in the crease of the goal. "She agreed to it all. We're going to leave next Friday so we can get there the night before the wedding."

"Holy shit," Simon whistles as Cam shakes his head. "Who's ready to start taking bets that this little fake relationship turns into something else?"

Hayden's hand darts into the air faster than everyone else's.

"Fuck the lot of you." I chuckle as I hit Simon in the helmet with my stick. "Nothing is going to happen between us."

"Mhm." Cam nods, rolling his eyes. "We'll see when you get back from Maine."

"Are you girls done gossiping and ready to practice?" Coach calls out across the ice to us. "Our last game before break is this weekend. So, let's get our shit together here. You guys can shoot the shit afterward."

I silently thank our coach for getting everyone back on track so they can stop busting my balls about Sydney. It's bad enough that I'm going to have her pretend to my family. I don't need all the guys on my case too, although it's completely expected from them.

We get back to practice and the guys are relentless as they take turns shooting their shots on goal. I attempt to block each shot, but my mind is definitely somewhere else right now. I'm already checked out and ready to get this winter break in full swing.

Which is completely weird.

I can't recall another time in my life where I was looking forward to something other than hockey...

———

The weekend flies by in what feels like faster than the blink of an eye. Our game goes without a hitch and even though I'm distracted, we still manage to win it. It was a nice little send-off before we have our break for Christmas. As soon as the holiday is over though, it's right back to the grind. And I'm weirdly looking forward to this break.

Something different, like a palate cleanser.

We don't have classes at all this week, since the semester ended. Most of the other students already cleared out and headed home early. Since I moved here my freshman year of college, this is already my home. And since the wedding is this weekend, I'll be spending more time in town than I have since my mom was diagnosed with cancer.

I feel pretty bad that I haven't been back to see her sooner, but that's life. And my life is here now. I am looking forward to going home and seeing her again. Especially with her being in better health now, although I know she's still pretty anxious about what is to come.

She of all people should know that we have no control over the future. And the only thing that we should be focusing our time and energy on is what we can control. I guess that's why she wants all of us to hurry up and get married. That is something she feels like she has some control over.

I spend most of the week just hanging with the guys and getting ready to go home. I spoke to Sydney earlier and she was practically ready to go already, just waiting until tomorrow. I told her that I would pick her up in the morning and we would begin our six-hour drive back to my hometown. She seemed nervous and excited, and there's a part of me that can't wait to show her my old stomping grounds.

None of this is real, though, and I have a feeling I might need to remind myself of that more often than not while we are away. It's weird, knowing I'm going to have to pretend that she's my girlfriend. I thought it was going to be simple, but I'm finding myself looking forward to things more than I should with her.

My phone begins to ring from my nightstand just as I climb into bed. As I pick it up, I notice my mother is calling and I accept the call before holding the phone to my ear.

"Hi, Ash," my mom says sweetly when I answer. "Are you getting your stuff ready to come visit?"

A soft chuckle slips from my lips. "I'm already packed and ready to go, Mom. Just waiting until the morning to start my drive."

"Oh, good," she says, clapping her hands together in excitement. "I can't wait to have all of my babies under the same roof again, even if it's only for one night."

"I know, I know. It's been a while since we've all been together like that." I pause for a moment, dropping down onto my mattress as I climb under the blankets. "How long are Catherine and Lucy staying?"

"They're both going to be staying until after Christmas. Andrew and Evelyn are leaving for their honeymoon the day after the wedding, so we won't be seeing them for Christmas."

I already knew this because my brother told me when I called to tell him that I was bringing a date. Both of my sisters are so far up my mother's ass, I'm not surprised they're sleeping at our parents' house, even though they both live in the same town as my mother.

"Andrew told me that you're bringing someone with you," she starts, her voice filled with hope and excitement. "When were you planning on telling me? I didn't know you had a girlfriend."

Swallowing roughly, I clear my throat. "Yeah, uh, her name is Sydney. I didn't want to tell you sooner and get your hopes up in case she wasn't able to come."

"What changed that she's coming now? The two of you are staying for Christmas too, right?"

"Yep," I tell her, sighing as I drop my head onto my pillow. "Her parents are traveling for the holiday, so she's able to stay with us. Just promise me that you're not going to be overbearing at all, please? We haven't been dating that long, so things are still new between us."

My mother laughs softly and a smile touches my lips at the sound. "Oh, honey. I won't scare her off, okay? Plus, this is the first time you've ever brought a girl home. The last thing I'm going to do is run her away."

"That's what I'm worried about," I mumble, closing my eyes as I inhale deeply. "Just be cool, Mom."

"I will, Asher." She pauses, laughing again. "Let me know when you're leaving in the morning. You know how I worry when you're traveling. Although... you won't be traveling alone this time."

Rolling my eyes, I purse my lips as I shake my head to myself. "Yes, Mother. I will let you know when I'm on the road. I love you and I'll see you tomorrow."

"I love you, honey. I can't wait to see you and meet the girl who finally managed to catch your eye."

We end the call and I toss my phone back onto my nightstand in exasperation. My mom doesn't usually annoy me and I honestly adore the woman, but I know how exhausting she can be too. I just need her to act normal and not freak Sydney out.

This is already a lot that I'm asking of her and she agreed to come meet my family.

Now, I just need them to all act normal and not scare Sydney away.

Easier said than done...

CHAPTER FOUR
SYDNEY

"Thank you again for agreeing to this," Asher says as he glances at me from the driver's seat. He came and picked me up this morning to start our road trip to Maine. And this might be the fourth time he's thanked me in the two hours we've been driving.

I can tell he's just as nervous as I am right now.

"You don't have to thank me, Ash," I tell him, offering a friendly smile as he looks back and forth between the road and me. "I have no problem helping a friend when they're in need."

Asher smiles before looking back at the road in front of him as we continue to speed down the free-way. "I really appreciate it. I just don't want my family to be too overbearing or anything. I told my mom that we haven't been dating that long, so we don't have to act like this is already an established relationship."

"I think I've known you long enough to be able to play the part," I tell him, picking at the cuticles of my nails. "You're a pretty simple person, Asher. I honestly feel like I'm at a bit of an advantage because of being friends with you for the past few years. You don't have anything to worry about. The whole thing will be totally believable."

"I hope so," he murmurs, his body swaying back and forth to the soft hum of the music that plays through the speakers. "I just want my mom to be proud of me for once, you know?"

"What happens after Christmas? We go back to life the way it was before, but what are you going to tell your family about us?"

Asher is silent for a moment, his jaw tightening as he effortlessly shifts lanes. "I don't know. I'll wait a little while to tell them, just so I don't kill my mother's joy too soon. And things just don't work out sometimes. Perhaps we both realized that we want different things in life."

A snort escapes me and I glance out the side window. "Well, that wouldn't be a lie," I mumble, more to myself than anything.

We fall back into the comfortable silence as we cross state lines, making our way closer to Asher's hometown in Maine. Grabbing the handle on the side of my seat, I put the back down and settle deeper into my seat with my pillow. Asher reaches into the back seat behind him and pulls out a blanket before handing it to me.

"We still have a few hours," he says softly, his lips tilting upward into a small smile. "Take a nap and I'll wake you when we get close."

"Thanks," I smile back at him, taking the blanket from him. My hand brushes against his and his warmth feels like an electric shock as it ripples along the nerves traveling up my arm. Asher stares at me for a moment, his eyes widening before he pulls his hand away from me and grips the steering wheel.

Turning away from him, I roll onto my opposite side and face the door. I cover my body with the blanket and hug my pillow to me as I close my eyes. It's hard trying to sleep, knowing that I'm trapped in this small space with him. He occupies too much of it, his scent overwhelming as it wraps itself around me. I bury my head into my pillow and wait for the car to lull me to sleep.

With the thoughts of my fake boyfriend drifting around in my head...

———

"Syd, hey," Asher's voice is soft as he lightly shakes my shoulder with his massive hand. "We're almost there."

Peeling open my eyes, I wipe a bead of drool away from the corner of my mouth. Lifting my head, I pull the pillow away and slowly sit up right as I put my seat back up. Asher is pulling his car down the street of a cookie-cutter development and I stare out the window, my eyes scanning the houses as we drive through.

They're all modest houses, nothing like what I grew up in, in California. Then again, my parents are loaded with more money than they know what to do with. And after living the extravagant life with the two of them, I wanted to get as far away from them as possible. Which is exactly what brought me to Wyncote University in Vermont. It was far enough away from them that I didn't have to continue living the same lifestyle and it was remote enough that I didn't know a single soul when I moved there.

I was able to create a life of my own—one where everyone didn't know that my father was one of the most powerful attorneys in the area. I didn't have to live up to the Phillips name. Instead, I was just

Sydney Phillips, your average student who was trying to complete a degree in psychology.

Asher never really talked much about where he came from. When his mother was diagnosed with breast cancer last year, he had confided in me about that, but that was as far as he went with divulging into his personal life. As we continue deeper into the neighborhood, I think it's safe to say that Asher's parents gave him a good life.

We pull into a cul-de-sac and he steers his car down the driveway of the largest house in the neighborhood. As a family of six, I can only imagine that they needed the space with all of the kids in the house.

"Is this where you grew up?" I ask Asher as he pulls his car behind one of the SUVs parked in the driveway.

He glances over at me as he puts it in park and nods. "We moved here after my younger brother was born. Our house before this one was much smaller, but my father had started his own construction business and it really took off. He actually had his crew build our house."

"That's really cool." I smile back at him, wishing I had some awesome story like that. I don't know. We lived in the Hills, in a house that was already constructed. My parents preferred to outsource everything, including having our house cleaned and our food cooked. God forbid that they lift a finger or get their hands dirty themselves.

"Yeah, I was really fortunate as a kid. I know that our house may not be much, but it was more than we ever needed. And they were able to pay for all of the extracurricular activities for four children and provide for us."

Tilting my head, I raise an eyebrow at Asher. "It's a lovely house, Ash. Seriously, I wish I lived in something like this and with an amazing family like yours."

"Didn't you live in, like, a five-thousand-square-foot house? And you think that this is lovely?"

A sad smile creeps onto my lips and I shrug. "Do you know how lonely a huge house like that is when you're an only child and your parents are too concerned with their own lives? I would have traded everything we had to have a family like this."

Asher is silent for a moment, his eyes scanning my face as he doesn't bother offering any bullshit words. There's nothing that he can say and there's nothing that I can do. We were both born into two different lives, but I want him to know that the monetary shit doesn't matter. The material things my family have don't matter to me, not when we didn't have a love like Asher's family does.

"You ready to get in there and meet everyone?" He shifts gears, changing the subject as he smiles at me. "I'm pretty sure Andrew and Evelyn are here, although Evelyn will be going and staying with her parents since the wedding is tomorrow."

"I'm ready." I grin at him, undoing my seat belt as I grab my purse and my pillow. Asher climbs out of the car, grabbing both of our bags from the back seat as I get out and follow after him. We walk up to the front door together and just as he's about to reach for the doorknob, it's pulled open.

A petite blonde woman, who looks exactly like her son, stands in front of us with a huge smile on her face. She pulls Asher in for a hug, wrapping her arms around him as she holds him for a moment before breaking apart. "How was your drive? No problems?"

"Nope." Asher smiles, shaking his head at her. "Mom, this is Sydney," he says, glancing back at me with the same smile that he gave her. "Syd, this is my mom, Rachel."

"Sydney," his mother beams at me, her eyes trailing over me as she steps toward me and pulls me in for a similar hug. "It is so nice to finally meet you. I always wondered what the girl who finally got my boy's attention would be like. I'm looking forward to getting to know you."

I choke out a laugh as it gets half caught in my throat, resembling more of a cough than anything. "I can promise you that I am nothing special." I laugh lightly, offering her a shy smile as we break apart.

"I highly doubt that," Rachel says, glancing back and forth between the two of us. Asher steps closer to me, wrapping his free arm around my shoulders. "Why don't the two of you take your stuff upstairs and meet the rest of us in the den? I apologize that we don't have any open guest rooms." Rachel offers the two of us a strained smile. "I know, bad mom to expect the two of you to sleep in the same bed, but you're both adults."

Asher falls tense beside me and he inhales sharply before glancing down at me with an apologetic look on his face. Rachel doesn't see the exchange between the two of us as she disappears inside the house, leaving Asher and me in the doorway.

"Shall we?" he says, his voice low and strained as he motions for me to go in through the door. I nod and step inside as he follows behind me, pulling the massive door shut.

The house is just as warm as Rachel's personality. It's decorated with various family pictures and different quote-type decorations. It matches their whole family vibe and is honestly exactly what I expected. I love it. I grew up in a house that had art hanging from the walls that were more expensive than other household items.

And I'm not saying that I'm ungrateful for that. My parents taught me a lot about art and different ways to interpret it and appreciate artists' talents. But this is what I always wanted. Somewhere that felt warm and safe. Like you could actually live in the house, not one that felt like it was staged and you couldn't get a fingerprint smudge on anything inside.

Asher heads up the staircase that leads to the second floor and I follow after him. He passes by all of the different doors, instead heading toward the back of the house to a door at the end of the hall. He slowly opens it and it reveals another staircase.

"My room is up here," he tells me, ducking his head slightly before he begins to make his way up the stairs. I follow after him, leaving the door open behind me as we head up into the attic. As we reach the top of the steps, it opens up into a huge room that expands over the top of the garage.

It looks like Asher hasn't changed his decor in here since high school. A queen-sized bed is situated in the middle of one wall, along with two dressers and a desk. A large TV hangs from the wall across from the bed. There aren't many decorations, but all of the ones that are hanging are either hockey pictures or a shelf full of trophies.

"Your mom didn't want to change this into a guest room or anything?" I question Asher as he drops both of our bags onto the bed.

He looks over at me, wincing slightly. "She struggled with empty nest syndrome when we all left. I think part of her didn't want to disturb any of our rooms in case we eventually came back. Although, she did change both of my sisters' rooms since they got married. I imagine that Andrew's room is next and then probably mine."

"That's actually really sweet," I tell him honestly. "You can tell how much she loves her family. And that's something you should never be embarrassed about."

Asher smiles at me and it's genuine. It touches his eyes, his dark gray irises dancing under the lights in his bedroom. "I'm sorry that we have to share a room," he offers softly, shrugging. "I can sleep on the floor and you can take the bed."

Tilting my head to the side, I raise an eyebrow at him. "Are you afraid to sleep in the same bed as me, Asher Golding?"

His throat bobs as he swallows hard, but he quickly recovers. A crooked grin works its way onto his lips. "Of course not. I'm just trying to be a gentleman here."

"So, we can both sleep in the same bed and nothing will happen. There's no sense in either of us being uncomfortable when there's plenty of room for the two of us in here."

"Are you sure?" he questions me, his voice hoarse and strained. Asher's eyes bounce back and forth between mine as he nervously shifts his weight on his feet.

"Yes, I'm sure." I pause, dropping my voice to a whisper. "This is just a fake relationship, remember? There's no reason either of us need to worry about something happening."

"You're right." He smiles, recovering from his nervousness. "If you decide to change your mind, I have no problem sleeping on the floor."

A laugh falls from my lips and I roll my eyes in exaggeration. "I'm holding you to your promise,

Ash. So, as long as you keep your word, then we don't have anything to worry about."

His head cocks to the side, an eyebrow raising as he stares at me for a moment. "You're something else, Syd." He pauses, chuckling softly as he motions back to the stairway that leads down to the second floor. "Ready to meet the rest of the family?"

A smile consumes my lips. "Let's do this."

CHAPTER FIVE
ASHER

Sydney has been taking everything in stride and I'm honestly so thankful for how well she adapts. She doesn't miss a beat and she's been playing the part of my girlfriend perfectly. No one seems to suspect a thing. Thankfully, she knows enough about me to be able to make it convincing that we recently started dating.

When they all ask how we met, she didn't lie as she told them that we met freshman year. She goes into great detail about our friendship and how it just transformed into something more without either of us realizing that it was happening.

Something about this just feels right and I don't know how to explain it. Sitting on the couch, with her tucked under my arm... it feels like this is exactly where she belongs. She's so comfortable around my family and they're all treating her like they've known her forever.

I don't know how to explain it, but it's definitely fucking with my head a little more than I want it to. Sydney is just a friend and I can't let anything mess that up. Even if my family is believing this little charade that we're playing.

"So, Sydney," my mother starts as she takes her seat back on the couch beside my father. "Asher told me that you'll be staying with us for Christmas?"

Taking a gulp of my wine, I pull my glass away from my lips and offer her a smile. "If you guys are sure that's okay. I don't want to impose on your family at all."

"Nonsense," my father says, shaking his head. "You're practically part of the family now."

Andrew stifles a laugh and my mother beams at the two of us, the pride exuding from her like no other. I hate being under their gaze right now, but it seems like we have everyone's attention in the room. Evelyn left after dinner to go back to stay with her parents and my sisters are well on their way to being wine drunk.

"Well, I think that it's probably time we head to bed. Right, babe?" I ask Sydney, tilting my head down to meet her eyes. She stares up at me, nodding along.

"Yeah, it's been a really long day and with the wedding tomorrow, we should probably get some rest."

"Of course." My mother smiles, rising to her feet as we both stand up. She pulls us each in for a hug, but she holds on to me longer as Sydney says her goodnights to everyone around the room. "She's a good one, Asher. Don't let this one get away."

My breath catches in my throat and I struggle to swallow past the lump that lodged itself there. The guilt of our facade weighs heavily on my shoulders, but I can't break my mother's heart now. She really likes Sydney—hell, they all do. And honestly, I'd be lying if I said I didn't feel the same exact way.

What the hell have I gotten myself into?

"I won't, Mom," I whisper, kissing her on the cheek before pulling away. Sydney stands at the other side of the room, a smile on her face as she watches the two of us. Her expression is infectious and as my eyes meet hers, I can't stop my lips from mimicking hers.

With everyone's eyes on us, I stride across the room to her, taking her hand in mine before leading her from the room. Her palm is warm, her fingers laced perfectly within mine. I don't let go of her hand as we walk through the house and up the stairs.

Slipping through my door, Sydney pulls it shut behind her as I lead her up to my bedroom. We both step into the space and for once, it feels like the walls are closing in on me. Sydney takes up so much space, draining the oxygen from the room. Turning on my heel, I stop as I face her. Her hand is still in mine, her chest rising and falling with each shallow breath as she tilts her head back to look at me.

Tonight with Sydney was something different, something I had never experienced with her before. Even though we were playing pretend, all of this felt like it was real. Like she's my real girlfriend instead of a fake one. And with the way she's looking at me right now, I want nothing more than to feel her lips against mine.

I've kept her in the friend zone for so long because I was afraid of what it would do to our friendship. And I was comfortable with the way things always were between us. That was before, and now I'm questioning it all.

Sydney clears her throat as she sucks her lips in between her teeth and shifts her weight nervously from foot to foot. "Um, I'm going to get changed and brush my teeth."

Ignoring the throbbing feeling inside my pants, I quickly drop her hand and take a step away from her. I don't know what the hell has come over me, but this shit needs to stop—like, now. I shouldn't be looking at her like this and my cock should definitely not be responding the way that it is.

"The bathroom is the second door on the right," I tell her, motioning to her bag. Sydney gives me a small smile and begins to go through her bag as she pulls out clothes. "I'll show you where it is so I can brush my teeth too."

"Thank you," she says softly as she grabs her toiletry bag and follows me back down the stairs. Everyone else is either still downstairs or already in bed, so the bathroom is empty as we reach it. Sydney slips inside and I wait for her to be finished. It doesn't take long before she's slipping through the door in an oversized t-shirt and a pair of shorts.

My breath catches in my throat as my eyes travel down her naked legs. This isn't my first time seeing Sydney in a pair of shorts, but it's like tonight, I'm seeing her under a completely different light. Seeing her dressed for bed is different than seeing her wearing a pair of shorts that everyone else can see her in.

It almost feels as if this look is reserved for just me right now.

"I'm going to brush my teeth and I'll meet you upstairs," I tell her, my voice strained and hoarse. My cock throbs in my pants and I quickly brush past her, the soft floral scent of her perfume invading my senses.

I don't wait for her to respond before I shut the door. Pressing my back against it, I fist my erection through my pants and wait for her footsteps to disappear up the stairs. I should just rub one out quick, get this out of my system so I can go to sleep and not have any lingering thoughts of my guest plaguing my mind.

Pushing off the door, I stride across the bathroom and stop in front of the sink. I stare at myself in the mirror, my dark gray irises almost appearing black from the amount of frustration building inside me right now. As badly as I want to just wrap my hand around my cock and forget about the girl waiting for me in my bed, I can't.

She's not waiting for me in that way either...

She's waiting for me to go to sleep, and that's it. No touching, no kissing. Just sleeping.

Running a frustrated hand through my hair, I let out a sigh before grabbing my toothbrush and toothpaste. I scrub them viciously, attempting to push away the unwarranted thoughts of Sydney. She's just a friend—one of my closest friends. I can't let my thoughts run rampant like this, not about her.

The last thing I'm going to do is let this fake relationship come between us.

After brushing my teeth, I head back into my room and find Sydney already tucked under the covers. She lifts her head when she hears me enter, her eyes meeting mine as she peeks from where she's situated in my bed.

Groaning inwardly, I walk over to the bed and grab my pillow as I look down at her for a moment.

"I wasn't sure which side was yours. Am I okay here?" she asks softly, her voice like velvet as it slides across my eardrums.

You're perfect, right where you are.

"You're fine," I tell her, obsessed with the way she looks in my bed. "I'm actually going to sleep on the floor, that way you can have the bed to yourself."

Sydney's eyebrows tug together and her face scrunches up as she looks up at me. "Are you sure? I don't mind sharing the bed or, if you prefer, I can sleep on the floor instead."

"Don't be ridiculous," I scoff, shaking my head at her as I grab the throw blanket from the end of the bed. I drop down onto the floor, situating myself on the plush rug that peeks out from under the frame. "You're my guest here. The last place you should be sleeping is on the floor."

"Asher," Sydney starts, her voice soft and quiet. "You don't have to sleep on the floor…"

"Don't, Syd." My words are strained as they get caught in my throat like peanut butter. Avoiding her gaze, I lay down and face the other way as I pull the blanket up to my chin. "Just go to sleep, okay?"

She's silent for a moment before I hear her whisper, "Okay." I know she was reluctant to agree, but it's better if she doesn't argue with me. Not right now.

If she tells me to get in that bed again, I don't know whether I'll be able to resist.

And it's better if we're like this… with as much distance between us as possible.

CHAPTER SIX
SYNDEY

When I wake up the next morning, Asher has already left and is starting his day. He's nowhere to be found in his room, but as I roll over in bed, I see a small piece of paper resting on the mattress beside my pillow.

Syd,
There's breakfast downstairs. I had to go help Andrew, but I will be back to pick you up this afternoon for the wedding. Make yourself at home.
-Asher

Reading his words warms my soul and brings a

smile to my lips, but I can't help but feel a little weird. I knew that he would have to be involved in the different wedding stuff today, especially since he's his brother's best man. However, I didn't really think about being alone at his home.

His family has been nothing short of welcoming and if I'm being honest, they've made me feel like I'm at home so far. But that doesn't make this any less weird. Damn Asher and him ditching me for the day.

I climb out of bed and grab my bag from the floor. Hoisting it onto the mattress, I find a pair of sweats and a sweatshirt to cover up with right now. It's almost eleven o'clock in the morning. The wedding isn't starting until four, but I would imagine that Asher should be here around two thirty or three to pick me up.

Even though he's in the wedding and I'm not, he's my ride there, so I have to go early and wait for the ceremony to start. I wonder if it's weird for his family. Sure, I'm his "girlfriend", but none of them know me. Is it weird that he brought me home for a family wedding and Christmas?

As I walk downstairs, I hear the sound of Christmas music playing from the kitchen. When I step inside the room, I see Rachel making gingerbread cookies. The scent drifts through the air, slipping into my nose as I inhale deeply.

"Good morning, Sydney!" she says brightly as she grabs a mimosa and hands it to me. "It's wedding day and so close to Christmas, so we're having quite the celebration today."

A laugh bubbles from my throat and I smile at her as she dances around the room in her Mrs. Claus apron. Her energy is infectious. My parents always celebrated Christmas, but they were never this into it. Asher's mom put a lot of time into all of her decorations throughout the house.

"There's some pancakes on the table if you want them. I'm just making gingerbread cookies because my mind needs to be preoccupied and I always make a bunch of cookies this time of the year."

I head over to the table and help myself to the food she has laid out. It appears that everyone else has already eaten. Glancing out into the den, I see Asher's two sisters sitting on the couch staring at the massive Christmas tree in the room.

"Don't mind the two of them," Rachel says as she comes over to me. "They're only fourteen months apart, so they've always been more like twins rather than regular siblings. I think they're both getting ready to go get their hair done. Did you want to come with us? We could see if one of the stylists could fit you in?"

"Aren't they in the wedding?" I ask her as I swallow a mouthful of pancakes and wash it down with the mimosa in my hand.

Rachel shakes her head. "No, Evelyn has her sisters and friends on her side. Which is fine, Catherine and Lucy don't mind. They've had their moment in the spotlight with their own weddings. Let me call the salon and see if we can get you in too."

I smile at her, not bothering to argue, even though I brought my own stuff to do my hair. Rachel doesn't seem like the type of person who is going to take no for an answer. And if I'm going to be at their house without Asher all evening, I might as well hang out with the girls if they'll have me.

―――

"Your hair looks amazing," Lucy beams as she stands behind me, fluffing the loose curls in the mirror. "Seriously, I would kill to have hair like yours."

Catherine and Lucy gush over the way that my hair curled and I couldn't be happier with how it turned out. Rachel, of course, insisted that she pay for everyone to get their hair done. I'll have to give Asher some money and he can make it seem like he's paying for it or something. I don't need his family doing extra little favors for me like this.

Just them inviting me along was nice enough.

We head back to the house and everyone goes their separate ways to get dressed. I hear Rachel and Dan, Asher's father, leave the house not long after they get ready. Both of his sisters leave with their husbands as well and I'm left alone in the house.

With it being winter, it's fairly cold, but thankfully the wedding will be inside, so I only have to worry about being cold while I'm outside. My dark wine-colored dress reaches my ankles, creating a waterfall of material down my legs. It hugs my curves around my torso and the long lace sleeves stop just at my wrists.

I bought the dress on a whim and this is the first time I'm wearing it. It's perfect for a winter wedding and matches the tie Asher said he had for his outfit. Even though I'm not in the wedding, we somehow managed to match anyway.

I hear his car pull up as I finish with one last swipe of mascara. I'm not sure what time he has to be back at the venue, so I quickly slip my feet into my heels and grab my clutch and peacoat before disappearing down the stairs.

As I reach the bottom of the stairs, I see Asher standing by the front door. His hands are shoved in the front pockets of his black dress pants as he leans against the doorframe. I pause for a moment, my eyes scanning him, dressed like I've never seen him before. A warmth spreads across the pit of my stomach and my heart pounds erratically in my chest.

His usually tousled hair is styled with not a single strand out of place. He lifts his head as he hears my heels on the wooden steps. I watch his throat bob as he swallows hard, his eyes widening slightly as his gaze travels up and down the length of my body.

Straightening my shoulders, I grab the handrail as I continue walking down the stairs toward him. Asher pushes away from the doorframe, pulling his hands from his pockets as he stares at me like he's completely transfixed. And the feeling is mutual. He looks fucking handsome as hell and I'm pretty positive my date might look better than the groom.

"Fuck, Syd," he murmurs, his words breathless as he meets me at the bottom of the stairs. He extends his arm, his hand reaching out for me. I slide my palm against his, letting him lead me down into the foyer. "You're absolutely beautiful."

Heat creeps up my neck, spreading across my cheeks as I'm trapped under his gaze. His words make my heart swell and I feel like the luckiest girl in the world with him right now. "Thank you," I practically whisper, instantly feeling shy. It isn't often that I get dressed up like this and to see how it's affecting him has me feeling confident as hell.

"Goddamn, I think I might have the hottest date at the wedding tonight." He pauses, flashing his white teeth at me as he grins. "Don't tell Evelyn, but you look even better than the bride does today."

"Oh, stop it," I giggle, pushing my hand against his chest. "You're a smooth talker, Golding, but remember, none of this is real."

His eyebrows tug together for a moment. "I don't give a shit. Tonight, I'm treating you like you're my real girlfriend. And I'm making sure every motherfucker in the building knows that you're mine."

He stares at me, his dark gray eyes staring directly through my soul. "And for the record, every word I say to you is real, Sydney. You're the most beautiful girl I've ever seen."

"Well, thank you." I smile back at him, releasing

his hand as he bends his arm for me to take it. "Shall we?"

"Hell yes." He grins as I slide my arm through his. "I'm ready to show you off to the rest of the guests. Let's just hope I don't get in any fights with anyone who decides to let their gaze linger too long."

Shaking my head, a light laughter falls from my lips as Asher leads me out into the cold afternoon air. Snow flurries spin around us and the chill in the air sends a ripple down my spine. "No fights, Asher. This is a wedding, not a hockey game. And just remember... even if their gazes linger too long, you're the one that I'm going home with."

I glance at him from the corner of my eye, watching the way his jaw tics. Last night was a little awkward with him sleeping on the floor, but there's been a weird shift in our friendship that I can't quite put my finger on. It's been my own little secret that I've had some budding feelings for him, but perhaps Asher Golding has a secret of his own, as well.

CHAPTER SEVEN
ASHER

At the altar, I stand beside my brother as a classical melody begins to play and Evelyn comes strolling down the aisle with her father. Everyone is on their feet, watching as the bride makes her presence known, heading directly toward Andrew. And as much as I try to keep my gaze on her, I can't help but find myself looking at Sydney through the crowd instead.

She's in the row with my two sisters and their husbands. She was reluctant at first because she isn't technically part of our family, but they insisted she sat with them. It warmed my heart at the way that they took her under their wing like this is where she belongs.

And I fucking hate the thought that next week,

all of this will be over. I thought that this little charade was only to appease my family, but I'm finding myself getting lost in the facade of it all.

Evelyn's father hands his daughter off to my brother and everyone takes their seats as the ceremony begins. They had everything planned so that it would be as quick and seamless as possible so we could get on to the reception. With it being four days before Christmas, their wedding was set with a winter theme and the snow falling outside really added to the whole vibe that they had going.

A smile touches my lips as I listen to them exchange their vows. And as sweet and touching as it is, I'm ready for this to be over so I can get back to my date. My brother and his fiancée finish their vows and the next thing I know, they're now husband and wife.

The crowd goes wild as they share their first kiss in front of everyone. I'm smiling and clapping, my eyes scanning the guests. My mother is standing with my father with tears streaming down the sides of her face. As I look past her, I meet Sydney's gaze. She smiles back at me, wiping at her own tears.

They begin to walk down the aisle as man and wife and the rest of us file out after them. Everyone is on their feet, already celebrating as we exit the building for pictures. I follow the rest of the wedding party, walking with Evelyn's sister who is her maid of honor as we go to a different area to get all of the photographs taken.

"So, I heard you brought a date," Evelyn's sister, Erin, says to me as she raises an eyebrow. From what I was told, she's single and she's also pretty attractive. But she doesn't come close to touching my girl. "Such a pity. I was hoping we could have had some fun tonight."

"Sorry," I give her a sympathetic smile as I shrug. "My girl is waiting for me when all of this shit is over. Although, I'm sure there's quite a few other single guys here."

"Meh." Erin purses her lips as she looks disinterested. "It's all good. I just heard enough about you that it's pretty surprising that you actually showed up with someone."

"That's me." I smile, winking at her as we line up for another picture. "I'm just full of surprises."

Erin breaks out into a laugh before we both get scolded by the photographer for not being ready for the pictures. Straightening my act up, I plaster my best smile onto my face as we go through the motions of getting the different photographs of the wedding party. I'm just ready for this to be over so the real fun can start.

After strolling into the ballroom, we all move along to the music as everyone is announced. Erin and I are the last ones and she drops it low on the floor, earning some hooting and hollering from the crowd as we take our places at the front. The DJ announces Andrew and Evelyn and they come strolling in, fist pumping as they walk into the room, hand in hand.

The music switches to a slow song, the one that Andrew and Evelyn chose for their first dance. Everyone rises to their feet, falling silent as the music plays and they take the center stage, sharing their first dance as man and wife. My eyes scan the crowd, landing on the table over to the side in the front of the ballroom where Sydney is standing as she watches them.

I can't take my eyes off her. It takes everything in me to not go over to her and sweep her off her feet. I want to spin her around the dance floor, to feel her arms linked around the back of my neck as my hands grip her waist. Our bodies moving in synchrony to the love song that plays.

Fuck. What the hell is happening to me? It must be the wedding atmosphere rubbing off on me because this is not what I'm about at all.

The newlyweds finish their dance, breaking apart as Andrew and my mother share their dance and then Evelyn and her father. Honestly, it feels like it's taking for-fucking-ever, but before I know it, it's over and people are crowding onto the dance floor. Thankfully, my brother and his wife decided to forgo any speeches and just wanted people to enjoy the rest of their night.

Personally, I think that they're pretty checked out from the whole process and are just ready to leave for their honeymoon to have some alone time.

I can't say that I blame them.

Pushing through the crowd, I head over to the table where my seat is. The same table that my girl is sitting at, waiting for me. Grabbing the chair, I pull it out and drop down onto it next to her. Sydney looks over at me, a bright smile on her face as her eyes shine back at me.

"That was a really beautiful ceremony," she says, raising her voice over the sound of the music that plays through the ballroom.

Gripping the back of her chair, I lean over, my lips brushing against her ear as I inhale her floral scent. "Nothing comes close to how beautiful you look right now."

Sydney inhales sharply and swallows roughly as I pull away from her. She grabs her glass of wine from the table and takes a long swig of it. A chuckle vibrates in my chest and I can't fight the grin that is on my face.

"You want to go to the bar and get a drink? I'm surprised you didn't get one during cocktail hour. It is an open bar, you know."

She tilts her head to the side, raising an eyebrow at me. "I wasn't sure if you were drinking tonight so I didn't want to be an embarrassment if I got a little tipsy."

"Babe, nothing you could do would ever embarrass me," I tell her, ignoring the fact that babe just rolled off my tongue like it was natural. "Plus, I started drinking before the ceremony."

Sydney takes the palm of her hand and drives it against my shoulder. "Not fair. I would have pregamed if I knew that was the deal." She pauses for a moment, abruptly rising from her seat before staring down at me expectantly. "Well, let's go get a drink then. It looks like I have some catching up to do."

Following her lead, I push my chair back and

stand up with her. Bending my elbow, I offer it to her and she slides her slender arm through mine. "You most definitely do. Let's go get you that drink and then maybe I can convince you to dance with me."

"I'm going to need a few drinks before you have a chance of that happening."

I have every plan of getting her out of her shell tonight.

But first, we'll start with a few drinks and getting her on the dance floor.

CHAPTER EIGHT
SYDNEY

The first few drinks go down with ease. We take a break from drinking when our meal is served, but it doesn't do much to diminish the buzz that I already have growing. I'm already pretty tipsy and feeling pretty good about it. Asher seems to be able to hold his liquor because he doesn't seem as drunk as I would imagine he would be right now.

The servers come around the table, clearing away our plates after we finish our meal. I'm feeling relatively stuffed, but I think that I'm finally ready to dance. The alcohol in my system has me loosened up and the DJ switches to a song that I absolutely love.

Pushing back my chair, I rise to my feet and hold my hand out for Asher. "Come dance with me?"

He raises an eyebrow, a sinister smirk playing on his lips as he takes my hand and slowly climbs out of his chair. He doesn't speak a word or bother to argue as I lead him out onto the dance floor. There's already quite the crowd out there, so it doesn't bother me dancing with all of these other people around. And not to mention, the alcohol. That gives me the confidence boost I need.

Asher moves in front of me as I begin to sway my hips to the beat. He's a pretty decent dancer and he doesn't once tear his eyes away from mine. I close the space between us, moving closer to him as he begins to move in tandem with me. Reaching out for him, I link my arms around the back of his neck.

His hands find my hips, his fingertips digging into my skin through the chiffon material of my dress as he pulls me closer to him. Our bodies are flush against one another, our hips moving together as we both sway to the music. Tilting my head back, I'm lost in the storm that brews in his dark irises.

Inside the storm, something else brews. He looks at me with pure unadulterated lust and I revel under his gaze. Maybe it's the alcohol or the boost of confidence he gives me. Either way, I feel his words coursing through my veins. That I'm the most beautiful girl he's ever seen.

Releasing my hands from around his neck, I slowly spin in his grip and his hands flatten along my stomach as I press my ass against him. His cock is hard, his erection pushing through his pants against me as I grind my hips. Working my body against him, he holds on to me as I lift my arms and link them back around the nape of his neck.

My back is flush against his firm chest and I'm lost in the feeling of him and the music that sounds throughout the room. I don't care if anyone is watching us and in this moment, I don't think that Asher really cares either. There's enough of a crowd around us, we're fairly hidden with the way that we're almost fucking through our clothes on the dance floor.

"Fuck, Syd," he murmurs in my ear, nipping at my bottom lobe. "You're driving me fucking insane."

"I thought this was all just pretend," I question him, unable to stop the words. They roll off my tongue and I blame it on the alcohol that completely dissolved my filter.

"I don't know what the hell this is anymore."

The lights above shift, dimming slightly as the music begins to shift into a slower melody. Asher's hands grip my hips as he spins me around to face him. I wrap my arms around the back of his neck as I face him, his hands gripping my waist as we sway back and forth to the slow song.

"I'm slow dancing in a fire of you, right now," he murmurs, dropping his face down to my neck. "And I want to fucking burn."

"You made me a promise," I whisper, my lips brushing against the side of his ear. "What about just being friends?"

"Fuck being friends," he growls as he nips at the skin along my neck. "You're my girlfriend until after Christmas, remember? We'll worry about what happens after it's over."

Swallowing roughly over the lump lodged in my throat, I nod, not fully trusting my voice. He's right. Even though none of this is real, that doesn't mean I can't enjoy myself and get lost in this pretend world that we've created. We'll worry about what happens after we go back to reality.

And hopefully our friendship won't be shattered like glass on the floor.

The night ends with everyone hooting and hollering as we send off the bride and the groom. Everyone is pretty tipsy by the end of the reception, thanks to the open bar that just kept the drinks flowing all night long. I'm feeling good as Asher and I walk hand in hand to the Uber that is taking us back to his parents' house.

Everyone ended up having to call Ubers because no one was really sober enough to drive. Asher mentioned to me that we would worry about his car tomorrow.

Asher helps me into the car and he slides into the back seat beside me. As I go to move to the other seat, he wraps his arm around my waist, holding me against him in the middle seat. I don't object because even though I know that this is wrong, I love the way that he feels with his side pressed against mine right now.

He doesn't let me go the entire time that we ride back to the house. When we arrive there, he slips the driver a twenty before helping me out of the car. I lose my balance on my heels momentarily and a giggle slips from my lips as Asher steadies me on my feet.

We stand on the sidewalk as the Uber pulls away, Asher still with his hands around my waist as snow continues to fall from the night sky above us. It's already created a thin layer on the ground and the concrete around us. Tilting my head back, I close my eyes and stick out my tongue.

"I love the snow," I breathe, opening my eyes as I watch my breath swirl in the chilly air. "There's something so peaceful and beautiful about it."

As I straighten my head, my gaze meets Asher's. The expression on his face is unreadable. His gray irises swirl with a fire that burns deep inside of them. He slowly moves one hand from my waist, reaching up as he cups the side of my face.

His warm palm is a stark contrast against my cool skin. He lightly strokes the pad of his thumb along my cheek, his head tipped down as his eyes slowly search mine.

"You've been right in front of me this entire time," he says softly, his voice hoarse as I get lost in the depths of his eyes. "How could I have possibly been so blind?"

My breath catches in my throat and a warmth spreads throughout my body. Asher's eyes drop down to my lips and I instinctively wet them with my tongue. He slowly moves his hand down to cup my chin as he runs his thumb across my bottom lip.

"I want to kiss you, Syd," he murmurs, his face dipping down to mine.

I stare back at him as he blinks once. "What are you waiting for?"

Asher claims my mouth with his own, his lips warm and soft against mine. My eyelids flutter shut and I'm lost in his touch as he steals the air from my lungs. This is all so wrong. We've gone well past playing the part of being in a fake relationship and now this is just clouding my brain.

It's too late for that, though. The alcohol and the entire night have transported us into a place that I never imagined we would be in. Our surroundings fade, the snow and the darkness of the night around us vanishing into thin air. Asher's tongue traces the seam of my lips and I part them, letting him in.

His kiss is soft and gentle, his tongue sliding against mine as I taste the liquor on his breath. Asher drains the oxygen from my lungs, his lips moving against mine in slow, sweet torture. I never imagined what it would be like to kiss him, but now that we're lost in this moment, my mind will never have to question it again.

His hand is warm against my face and he slowly breaks away from me, both of us coming up for air. He leaves me breathless, my chest rising and falling with every shallow breath I take. My heart pounds erratically in its cage and I desperately want to feel his lips against mine again.

"Syd," he murmurs, his voice soft like silk against my eardrums. "Let's get you inside before you turn into an icicle out here."

I nod, not fully trusting my voice as he steps away from me. A rush of cold air replaces his warmth, sending a shiver down my spine. I want to feel him close to me again, but instead, he slides his hand in mine. Our fingers are laced together as he leads me into the warmth of his home.

The house is already quiet with everyone tucked away in their beds for the night. It was a long day with the wedding and after all of the partying and alcohol, I'm sure they were all exhausted.

My body sways, high from the liquor and his kiss, as he leads me up the two flights of stairs until we reach the third floor. Asher pulls the door shut behind us as he leads me into his bedroom. He flips the switch on the wall and slides it down as he dims the lights in his room.

Asher leads me into the center of his room, releasing my hand as he walks over to his dresser. I watch him as he pulls out a pair of sweatpants and turns to face me. His expression is unreadable, almost as if he's unsure of what move to make next.

There was a shift from our kiss outside. The tension in the air is palpable and I want to wash it all away. Kicking off my heels, I push them over toward my bag before I walk over to his bed and drop down on the mattress. Asher leans against his dresser as he pulls off his tie and begins to work his fingers on the buttons of his dress shirt.

"I know today was a long day and we should probably get some sleep, especially after all of the drinking we did tonight."

I stare back at him, my eyes transfixed on the way he slides the buttons through the holes of his shirt. My breath catches in my throat as I watch him shrug his shirt over his shoulders, letting it fall to the floor. His body is perfectly sculpted and my eyes travel over the curves and planes of his muscular form.

"I don't really feel as drunk as I did earlier," I admit quietly as I rise to my feet. Asher's eyes are on mine as I hook my fingers under the straps of my dress. "And I'm not sure I'm ready to go to sleep yet."

"No?" he questions me, tilting his head to the side as he raises an eyebrow. "Well, what did you have in mind?"

The corners of my lips lift. "For starters, you're not sleeping on the floor again tonight." I pause, slowly pushing the straps down my arms. My dress begins to slip from my body and I push it down, letting it fall down my torso and then my legs before pooling on the floor around my feet.

"And where am I going to sleep?" he questions me as he begins to stalk across the room toward me. A fire burns in his irises as his eyes trail over my half-naked body.

"In your bed with me."

CHAPTER NINE
ASHER

*F*uck.

Sydney stands in front of me in just her bra and underwear and I'm ready to strip her naked and toss her onto my bed before burying myself deep inside her. I don't bother hiding my cock that is as hard as a rock in my dress pants.

"And what happens then? We sleep?"

A playful smirk teases her lips and she shakes her head as I step into her space. I stop as my toes touch hers, sliding my hand around the back of her neck as she tilts her head up to look at me. "I told you, I'm not ready to go to sleep."

"So, what do you want to do then, babe?"

She slides her hands across my naked chest, dragging her nails along my skin as she looks up at me. Her plump lips are still red from when I kissed her outside and it's taking everything in me not to claim them with my own again.

"Come to bed with me and find out."

Sydney reaches for me, hooking her fingers in the belt loops of my pants as she walks backward, stepping out of her dress, toward my bed. The backs of her knees hit the mattress and she drops down onto it, parting her legs as she pulls me closer to her. Grabbing my belt, she slides it through the metal clasp and undoes it before reaching for the button of my pants.

Sliding my hand along her scalp, my fingers slide through her long locks of hair as she unbuttons my pants and slides down the zipper. My cock throbs, straining against my boxers as she slowly begins to push down my dress pants. They're halfway down my thighs before she hooks her fingers under the waistband of my underwear and begins to push them down too.

Using one hand to push down my boxers, she slides the other along the bottom of my abdomen before sliding down to my groin. My cock is freed from my underwear and Sydney wraps her delicate hand around the shaft. Gripping it at the base, she slowly moves her palm along my dick. Tilting her head back, she stares up at me through her long black eyelashes, batting them in a bashful way.

"What are you up to, Syd?"

A smirk plays on her lips as she continues to stroke my cock with her hand. "You're my boyfriend for the next week, right?"

Swallowing roughly over the lump in my throat, I nod.

"Then I'm going to take care of you." She pauses for a moment, licking her lips as she stops with her hand wrapped around my shaft. "I want to make you feel good, Asher."

Her lips part slightly, her mouth opening wider as she wraps them around the head of my cock. A moan vibrates in my chest, my balls instantly tightening from the sensation of her soft, warm mouth. She runs her tongue along the underside of my dick as she bobs her head, inhaling me until her lips reach her hand.

She drops her hand for a moment, sucking me in deeper until the tip of my cock is hitting the back of her throat. She gags slightly, choking on my length before sliding her mouth back along my shaft. Wrapping her hand around the base, she moves it along with her mouth, bobbing back and forth as she sucks my cock.

I've gotten head from plenty of girls before, but fuck, they've never felt as good as she does right now. Wrapping my hands in her hair, I grip the long locks tightly as she fucks me with her mouth. Her head bobs faster, her hand moving in a perfect rhythm with it as she continues to suck me in and out of her mouth.

My head falls backward, my eyes screwing shut as I'm lost in pure rapture with this girl. Sydney has been one of my closest friends and sure, the thought had crossed my mind before, but I never actually considered crossing the line. I never wanted to ruin our friendship, but I think it's too late to worry about that right now.

I don't know what will happen after we go back to reality, but for now, I'm going to enjoy every moment that I have with this girl.

Sydney continues to bob her head, moving faster as she runs her tongue along the underside of my cock. My balls constrict, drawing closer to my body as I'm nearing my release.

"I'm going to come, Syd," I groan, feeling the warmth spreading through my body as she pushes me closer and closer to the edge. Instead of stopping, she goes harder, and that's all it takes to have me falling off the cliff, straight into an abyss of ecstasy.

I lose myself in her, coming in her mouth as she continues to suck me dry. My orgasm tears through my body and I feel like I could collapse from the euphoria that fucks my system. Sydney moves her head slower, her lips popping as she releases my cock from her mouth. I watch her throat bob as she swallows and I swear to God, it feels like my dick is getting hard already.

A smile lifts the corners of her lips as she wipes her mouth with the back of her hand. I slowly release the grip I have on her hair and run my hands down the sides of her neck. As I reach her chest, I move around her back and unclasp her bra before peeling it from her body.

I toss it onto the floor and leave my pants by her dress as I push her back onto the bed. Her head hits the mattress, her hair fanning out around the top of her head like a halo as I climb over the top of her. My lips find hers in an instant. Sydney wraps her arms around the back of my neck as our tongues dance with each other's.

Pulling away from her, I start at her jawline, trailing my lips down to her neck. My tongue slips out and I drag it down the length of her throat before nipping at her skin at the base. Sydney's hands find my shoulders, her nails digging into my skin as I continue my journey across her body. Sucking and tasting her flesh as I make my way to her breasts.

I bring my mouth to her nipple, pulling her puckered flesh between my teeth. I wrap my hand around her other breast, kneading her flesh with my fingers as I suck and lick her tit. A moan slips from her lips, her body writhing under my touch. Abandoning the right one, I switch to the other, mimicking the same assault with my mouth.

Moving down farther, I slide down the bed as I move my lips along her torso. As I reach her legs, I hook my fingers under the waistband of her panties and remove them from her. Pushing apart her legs, I settle between her thighs and lift my eyes to hers. I meet Sydney's gaze as she lifts her head and stares down at me.

"What are you doing?" she murmurs, her voice thick with need.

Winking at her, I lick my lips. "Repaying the favor, beautiful girl."

I slide my tongue along her pussy, starting from the bottom until I reach her clit. Glancing up at her, I watch her head fall back onto the bed as a moan slips from her lips. Her hands find my head, sliding through my hair as she grips on the strands.

A smile forms on my lips before I suction them back to her pretty pussy. She tastes fucking sweet—like goddamn candy. I swipe her again with my tongue before circling around her clit. Sydney grips tightly on my hair as I continue to eat her pussy like it's my last meal.

Moving my tongue against her, I continue the same motions before landing on her clit. Her hips buck and I pin her legs down with my arms as I flatten my tongue and press it against her clit. Rolling it back and forth, I apply more pressure, swirling around the bundle of nerves.

"Oh my god," she moans, fighting against me as she attempts to lift her hips. I chuckle, the sound vibrating against her pussy before I circle her clit again. Flicking my tongue harder and faster, it isn't long before she's reaching her peak.

I can feel her arousal building as her legs begin to shake and I push her over the edge. She's falling into the abyss of ecstasy as her orgasm tears through her body. She moans my name loudly, withering under my mouth as I continue to lick and taste every last drop of her.

She rides out her high, her body shaking underneath me as I suck her lips into my mouth, getting one last taste before I pull away. Lifting my head, I move up on the bed and settle between her legs. My cock is already hard again and she stares up at me with a hooded gaze. The euphoria is coursing through her veins and she gives me a lazy smile.

"Jesus Christ, Asher," she murmurs, her voice breathless. "That was fucking amazing."

A smirk forms on my lips. "That was just the start, Sydney... I'm nowhere close to being finished with you."

CHAPTER TEN
SYDNEY

A smirk plays on Asher's lips as he climbs over the length of my body. My legs are already splayed out on the bed as he settles between them. Asher hovers over me, his face just inches from mine as he plants his hands on the bed beside my head.

I watch as his expression changes, the smirk falling from his lips as his eyes slowly search mine. A wave of emotion passes through them and I desperately want to know what's going through his head right now. Instead, he stares down at me, silent and unmoving.

"You're fucking beautiful, Sydney," he murmurs, his eyes shining back at me as his gaze penetrates mine. "Seeing you like this has my heart feeling like it's about to combust."

My throat is thick with emotion as I wrap my hands around the back of his neck, pulling his face down to mine. We've both had enough to drink tonight, but I think we're sober enough that we shouldn't be having this conversation. Nothing with emotion is good for us. And Asher is kicking things up a notch.

I can't have him under my skin, getting in my head and playing with my emotions. We need this to be mindless, just two friends enjoying each other —nothing more.

Asher's mouth collides with mine, his tongue instantly parting my lips as he slips it inside. My head swims as he kisses me senseless, stealing the air from my lungs as our tongues tangle together. He distracts the thoughts from my mind, pushing them far away as I focus on the way his body feels pressed against mine.

The tip of his cock presses against my center and I roll my hips, inviting him in. I'm on birth control, so there's no need for a condom or any worry of pregnancy. And God knows, I'm not stopping him in this moment to have that goddamn awkward conversation.

Asher leaves one hand on the bed beside my head as he slowly begins to move his hips, sliding inside me. His other hand trails down my body, sliding under my ass as he lifts me up to get a better angle. His grip tightens on my flesh as he fills me completely. Asher moans into my mouth and I swallow the sound, a smile playing on my lips.

It's insane, knowing that I have this effect on him. Never once in my life did I ever think that we would actually end up in bed together. But here we are... and here he is, acting like I've always wanted him to. Just knowing that he's this into it has me ready to lose myself around him already.

His lips leave mine, trailing along my jawline and down my neck as he begins to move his hips in a steady pace. He rocks in and out of me, his cock stroking my insides as he dives in deep with every thrust. My body is still on fire from him going down on me and I don't know how much more I can take of this.

Asher's mouth is on my throat, licking and sucking my skin as his hand grips my ass tightly. He lifts me up every time he thrusts into me, but instead of picking up the pace, he slows it down. It's almost goddamn torturous because I just want him to fuck me into oblivion at this point. Instead, he's teasing me, slowly easing his cock in and out.

"What are you doing?" I murmur, sliding my hands into his hair. Wrapping my fingers around his locks, I pull his face away from my neck until he's lifting his head and looking back at me.

A sinister smirk plays on his lips. "Taking my sweet time with you."

I shake my head, biting my lip as he thrusts into me harder the next time he moves his hips. "I want you to fuck me, Asher. Fuck me until the world around us ceases to exist."

"I will, beautiful," he breathes, his lips finding mine in a slow kiss before he pulls away again. "I'm not ready to be done with you, though."

I look up at him, tightening my grip on his hair. "This is goddamn torture," I practically plead, my voice sounding more like a whimper than anything. "Fuck me, Asher. Fuck me like you mean it."

He doesn't say another word, instead a peculiar look mixes with the fire burning in his irises. Thrusting his hips, he slams into me and I can't stop the moan from slipping from my lips. A smirk plays on his and he stops with his cock fully inside me.

"Is that what you want, Sydney?" he questions

me, tilting his head to the side as he raises an eyebrow. "I'll give you whatever it is that you want, babe."

I nod. "Please, Asher."

Asher pulls his hand away from my ass, planting it back on the bed as he slowly moves his hips. He begins to pull out of me and just when I think that he's going to stop with the tip inside of me like he has been, he doesn't, instead he completely pulls out of me and I feel his absence immediately.

Pushing my bottom lip out into a pout, I stare up at him in confusion. The cold air from the room takes the place of his warmth and I find myself reaching for him, trying to pull him back to me. A chuckle vibrates in his chest as he smacks my hands away, rising to his feet. He stands by the edge of the bed, staring down at me for a moment.

My lips part as I begin to protest whatever the hell he's doing. This is the complete opposite of what I asked, and he said he would give me whatever I want. As I'm about to question him, he wraps his hands around my ankles and quickly pulls on my legs, dragging me down to the edge of the bed with him.

A yelp escapes me, as his movements startle me.

Asher stares down at me with that same damn smirk on his lips. "What? Did you think I was just going to leave you like that?"

"I don't know what the hell you're doing," I breathe, attempting to lift myself up on my elbows. Asher is faster than me, planting his hands on my collarbones as he pushes me back onto the bed.

My heart pounds erratically in my chest, my breathing rapid and shallow. My need for him is greater than anything I've ever felt before. Warmth floods me as I stare up at the fire burning in his eyes. Asher reaches for me, his hands finding my waist. His fingertips dig into my flesh as he abruptly flips me onto my stomach.

There's something about this side of him that is driving me wild. I like him like this, taking complete control. I've never seen this Asher before, but I fucking love it.

I'm on the bed on my stomach and Asher's hands slide down to my hips. Gripping them, he lifts my ass into the air, positioning himself behind me at the same time. The head of his cock presses against me, but he doesn't fully enter me.

He releases my hip with one hand and slides it down the length of my spine. I feel his hands in my hair as he wraps the length around his fist and tugs lightly. "Tell me what you want, Sydney."

Swallowing roughly, I glance at him over my shoulder. "I want you to fuck me, Asher. Hard."

A feral groan slips from his lips and he abruptly thrusts his hips, slamming his cock into me. I cry out, partly in surprise and partially from the pleasure coursing through me. He tugs on my hair and grips my hip with his other hand as he begins to pound into me.

There's no gentleness in his touch anymore. All that's left between us is the need for release. He does exactly what I ask, fucking me harder and harder with every thrust. I can barely hold myself up and I don't even know what sounds are escaping me anymore. I can't stop moaning as he strokes my insides with his cock, pushing me closer and closer to the edge.

He tightens his grip on my hair as my pussy clenches around him. "Come for me, beautiful," he growls, his fingertips digging into the flesh of my ass.

That's all it takes. His command, his balls slapping against me, and one last thrust as he fills me completely. I shatter around him, losing myself in nirvana as my orgasm tears through my body. My legs shake, my pussy clenching harder around him as my body ignites on fire.

Asher isn't far behind me, pulling out at the last minute as he coats my ass with his cum. I feel the warmth, the sound of his groans as he comes. I can no longer hold my body up as I collapse onto the mattress. My chest heaves, rising and falling with every shallow breath I take.

He disappears for a moment, before he's wiping the mess from my backside with an article of clothing. My heart pounds erratically as I try to catch my breath. I'm still riding out my high, my head swimming from the current state of ecstasy that he induced in me.

I slowly climb up the length of the bed, collapsing again as I reach the pillows. Asher pulls the covers back and slips in underneath them as he positions the sheets over the two of us. He slides his arm under my neck, pulling me flush against his side as he lays on his back.

Resting my cheek on his chest, I listen to the sound of his heart beating erratically against its cage. Neither of us say a word, and honestly, I don't think any are needed in this moment. I don't want this night to be over, but I can barely hold my eyelids open as exhaustion begins to set in.

"Sleep, my beautiful girl," Asher murmurs as he plants his lips against my forehead.

He warms my soul with the warmth of his mouth and I never want to let him go.

But I know this can never happen again.

And I'm afraid for what tomorrow will bring.

CHAPTER ELEVEN
ASHER

I feel her warmth against me before I even open my eyes. Her breathing is still shallow, her chest rising and falling with every soft snore that slips from her lips. Slowly opening my eyes, I blink rapidly against the harsh morning sun that shines through the window.

Sydney stirs slightly in her sleep, her naked body pressed against mine. My arms are still wrapped around her, holding her tightly as the night before plays over in my mind. Dancing with her at my brother's wedding, bringing her back to my parents' house, and sharing a bed with her.

We crossed a line that I had never intended on crossing and there was no going back from it now.

Slowly sliding my arm from under her neck, I

roll away from her, careful to not disturb her as she continues to sleep. My head is pounding, I need to take a piss and get something to drink. After the alcohol we consumed at the wedding last night, I'm sure Sydney is going to be feeling like shit when she wakes up too.

She doesn't stir as I slip out of the room and softly close the door behind me. The smell of pancakes and bacon drifts up the stairs, coming from the kitchen downstairs. My stomach growls and I slip into the bathroom to relieve myself. After washing my hands and brushing my teeth, I head downstairs, where I find my mother already making breakfast.

No one else is in the kitchen with her and I pour myself a cup of coffee before dropping down onto one of the barstools at the island.

"Rough night?" she questions me as she slides a plate with some food on it in front of me. I don't miss the twinkle in her eye and the smirk that twitches the corners of her lips. "I spoke to your brother this morning and he and Evelyn were getting ready to board their plane to Hawaii."

"Is he going to let you know when they land?"

Knowing my mother, I'm sure she's already given him the rundown of how he needs to let her know that they get there safely. I can't fault her for it. Her children have always been her life and after her cancer diagnosis, it's like she's been looking mortality in the face ever since.

She confirms what I already knew and we chat about Christmas plans as I finish my breakfast. Since the holiday is only three days away, my mother is already preparing and making sure that everything will be ready. There's a sadness to her when she speaks of it, since my little brother will be missing the day with us, but she seems happy enough that the rest of her family is here.

As she slips out of the kitchen, I grab a clean plate and pile some food on it before pouring Sydney a cup of coffee. She hasn't come out of my bedroom yet and I don't know if she's still sleeping or if she might feel a little uncomfortable just walking down here. So, I decide to take her breakfast in bed instead.

When I reach my bedroom and slip inside, Sydney is already awake and out of bed. She pulls her shirt over her head, quickly slipping her arms through the holes as I stride into my room. Her face is bright red as she spins on her heel, covering her body as if I didn't see every inch of her skin last night.

"You hungry?" I ask her, a grin tugging on the corners of my lips at her sudden shyness. My eyes search her face, looking for any hint of regret, but if she's feeling it, she's concealing it pretty well.

Sydney lifts her eyes to mine, a smile playing on her lips. I watch her eyes as they widen when they drop down to the plate in my hand and she eagerly nods. "I'm literally starving and my head is killing me right now."

I motion for her to sit down on the bed and she follows suit, sitting cross-legged as I set the plate in front of her and hand her the cup of coffee. I watch her as she wraps her hands around the warm mug and brings it to her plump lips, taking a sip before she gives me a look of pure satisfaction.

"Damn, Golding, you know the way straight to my heart."

My breath catches in my throat from her words, but I quickly force myself to breathe as I sit down on the bed beside her. "We need to talk about last night."

Sydney glances over at me as she shoves a piece of pancake into her mouth. Her eyes widen slightly, bouncing back and forth between mine before she washes down her food with a sip of coffee. "What do we need to talk about? We were both drunk and it happened."

"I know and I wanted to apologize to you for it," I tell her, my voice hoarse as I choke out the words. Her eyes narrow slightly. "I don't want you to feel like I took advantage of you or anything because of the state we were both in. And I don't want to ruin our friendship because of it."

Sydney tilts her head to the side, raising an eyebrow at me. "Asher, I wasn't that drunk. I knew the decision that I was making, so it isn't all on you. And I agree. I don't want our friendship to suffer because we got drunk and messed around."

I stare at her for a moment as she directs her attention back to the food in front of her. Words fail me in this moment and the tension hangs heavily in the air between us. There's a shift in our friendship now, whether either of us want to admit it.

You can be the best of friends with someone, but once you see each other naked, everything changes. I've tasted and touched her in ways I never have before. I've been balls deep inside of her. How the fuck are we supposed to just go back to the way things were before, like none of this ever actually happened?

I can't tell if Sydney really agrees with what I

said about not ruining our friendship or if she's just agreeing with me because she doesn't want to be the one to cause any ripples in the water. I don't know how the hell to proceed, but I guess the only way I can is by pretending things are back to the way they were before.

That should be easy, right?

I mean, Sydney was one of my closest friends before we ended up in bed together. All I have to do is push the memories from my mind and get things back to the way they were before. Our friendship can still recover from this. It's not over between us, and that thought brings me a little bit of relief...

Even if it's as much of a lie as our fake relationship.

CHAPTER TWELVE
SYDNEY

Asher has been doing his best to try and make things seem like they're back to the way they were before last night. I've been trying to let him distract me in an effort to force my brain to go back to focusing on our friendship. I don't regret what happened between the two of us. It was honestly better than I ever imagined— but I don't want to lose Asher as a friend.

And that's the only way he'll be in my life. He's made it clear from day one that he doesn't do relationships. So, I've let him keep me in the friend zone, even though we crossed that clear line last night. That doesn't change anything between us, though. My mind and my heart need to get on the same page about that.

Because now my thoughts about him are more clouded than they've ever been.

Asher pulls his car up outside of the outdoor ice rink. The parking lot is relatively full and Christmas lights are strung between the lamps that light up the lot. He insisted on going ice skating this evening, after we spent all afternoon helping his mom bake more Christmas cookies.

I swear, if that woman bakes any more, they're going to be eating cookies until next Christmas.

"So, I need to tell you something," I tell Asher as we both climb out of his car and begin to walk over to the booth that is near the entrance to the rink. My stomach is in knots and my anxiety is making me want to dig my heels into the snow-covered ground. "I've never been ice skating before and I'm actually pretty scared to do it."

Asher stops in his tracks, turning to look at me as his eyebrows tug together. "Like, not even when you were a kid?"

I shake my head, stopping beside him. He's at least a foot taller than me, so I tilt my head back to look up into his gaze. "My parents weren't really into doing family activities like that. And I think it may have snowed, like, twice my entire life where we lived."

"You don't have to be afraid," he tells me, a grin tugging at the corners of his lips. "I don't know if you know this or not, but I spend a lot of time on the ice. I won't let you fall."

I swallow hard, his words hanging heavily in the cool air between us.

I'm terrified of falling... and I don't mean on the ice.

"Come on," he says, his gloved hand warm as he wraps it around mine and begins to drag me closer to the rink. "I'll help you, okay?"

I let Asher lead me over to the booth where he pays for both of us. He gets a pair of white skates for me and walks over to a bench for us to get our skates on. I take a seat, slipping my feet from my shoes as Asher sits down beside me. He brought his own skates with him and quickly laces them, while I'm still getting my feet in mine.

He looks over at me, flashing his bright white teeth as he shifts his body and crouches down in front of me. "Let me help you."

Swallowing roughly over the lump lodged in my throat, I nod, releasing the laces as he takes them in his own hands. He starts at the bottom, pulling them tightly as he works his way up. As he begins to loop them through the hooks, he glances up at me, his eyes glimmering under the Christmas lights above us.

"Do they feel like they're tight enough?" he asks, pulling on them once more before he begins to tie them. "You always want to make sure that they're secure enough to provide more stability for your ankles."

"They feel tight," I tell him, my voice barely audible as I remind myself that all of this is fake. He's just helping a friend tie her ice skates. Nothing more and nothing less.

Asher finishes and helps me to my feet as he laces his fingers with mine again. He leads me over to the entrance of the rink and stops. Using his other hand, he slides the protectors off his skates and steps out onto the ice. His hand is still in mine and he gently pulls me along with him, helping me as I enter the rink.

It feels unnatural and abnormal, like I have absolutely no control over how my feet are moving. I struggle to gain my footing, feeling my legs move as my feet begin to slide on the ice. It's slippery as hell and I don't know what to do. My heart pounds erratically in my chest and panic builds in the pit of my stomach.

Asher is still holding my hand, but I quickly drop

it and grab onto his biceps for more support. A soft chuckle vibrates in his chest, his hands finding my hips as he tries to steady me. "You're good, Syd. I got you."

The panic is building and I want nothing more than to feel the normal ground under my feet instead of ice. "I can't do this, Asher. I'm going to fall and bust my ass."

"No, you're not," he laughs, his eyes twinkling under the lights above. "You just need to get your feet steady underneath you. I'll help you and I promise I won't let you fall. Do you trust me?"

I nod, inhaling deeply through my nose as I try to control my breathing. It's a weird feeling, like I'm not in control of my own balance right now and for whatever reason, it almost brought on a full-blown panic attack. But I do trust Asher. I trust him to keep me safe, even if it means that my heart is in danger.

Asher waits for me to get my balance and my fingers dig into his flesh as my feet begin to slide again without my direction. "Here," he says softly, wrapping his hands around mine as he pulls them away from my hips. "I'm going to help you."

"Wait, why are you making me let you go?" I question him, my words coming out in a rush as I notice my breath in the air. "I need to hold on to you."

Asher laughs softly again as he moves behind me. His hands find my waist and he holds on to me tightly. "I'm not going to let you go, Syd. Just do exactly what I tell you to do. You need your hands free to use your arms to gain balance."

"This was a terrible idea, Asher. Can we just go back?"

"Nope," he says matter-of-factly. "We're already here, babe. It's scary trying new things, but are you really living if you're not trying something new? We'll go around once and if you absolutely hate it, then we can be done."

An exasperated sigh slips from my lips and I glance at him over my shoulder, feeling the panic as it races through my veins. "Fine. What do I do?"

"I'll help you move, but start off by slowly gliding your feet. One at a time. Push one forward and push off with your opposite foot until you're shifting your weight back and forth."

I try to make sense of his words but get tripped up as I try to move my feet the way he just instructed. Asher pushes me along, moving his skates effortlessly as I attempt to mimic the same action. It's not as easy as he makes it seem, but I'm determined to do exactly what he said. There's nothing wrong with trying new things and I need to live a little.

"See, you're getting it," Asher breathes softly in my ear. "I'm going to let go of your waist and move beside you, is that okay?"

"I don't know," I choke out, feeling the anxiousness again at the thought of doing it by myself.

"You can do it, Syd," he whispers, his lips brushing against the shell of my ear. His breath is warm on my neck and a shiver slides up my spine. "I'll be right here beside you. Believe in yourself the way that I believe in you."

"Easy for you to say," I mumble, shaking my head as Asher pulls me to a stop. My stomach rolls and my legs shake as he lets go of me and moves beside me. "You practically live on ice skates, so this is like riding a bike for you."

Asher chuckles softly, wrapping his hand around mine. "I don't know when the last time was that I rode a bike. I don't think that would be a pretty sight."

"Tell you what," I respond, my voice shaking as Asher begins to move the two of us across the ice. My feet feel weird and my legs feel unnatural as I attempt to move them back and forth in the way he told me to. "Since I agreed to do this with you, you need to agree to riding bikes with me sometime."

"You do know that it's the middle of winter and it snows pretty often, right?" he questions me, tilting his head down as he gives me a crooked grin.

A laugh bubbles from my throat and I shake my head at him as the panic begins to ease from my system. I'm starting to feel a little more comfortable the more we move, and knowing that he has my hand in his gives me a peace of mind. I trust him to catch me if I fall.

"In the summer then? You owe me a bike riding date."

Something unreadable shimmers in his eyes and he stares down at me for a moment. "You've got yourself a deal, Phillips."

I smile back at him, feeling the warmth spreading through my body as he squeezes my hand. Snow begins to fall, the white flurries drifting around us as Asher continues to help me as we move around the circle. Other people skate past us and I know that Asher could easily outskate any of them, but instead he chooses to be with me.

It's a magical moment. The snow falling, Christmas lights hanging above, and the soft classical holiday tunes playing from the speakers that are lined around the rink. It feels like a moment straight out of a holiday movie, but it's not. This is all real.

The thought of being Asher's fake girlfriend doesn't even enter my mind. Instead, we're both lost in the moment together, hanging on to every minute that we have together like this. His palm warms mine through our gloves and I begin to skate with more ease with him.

"Thank you for being here with me tonight," Asher says softly as he turns to face me, sliding effortlessly on his skates.

I attempt to turn to face him and my feet begin to shift faster than I want them to. My hand flies out of his, my arms flinging into the air as my legs begin to wobble and slide out from under me. I yelp as I lose my footing, but Asher's hands dart out and he grabs me before I hit the ice.

He holds me upright, helping me straighten out as he wraps his hands around my waist. My hands find his shoulders and I tilt my head back to look up at him, my heart pounding erratically in my chest. Losing my footing scared me—I thought for sure I was going to fall.

But Asher kept his word. He promised he

wouldn't let that happen and he was sure to catch me before I busted my ass.

Moving one hand from my waist, he slides his gloved hand along the side of my face as he cups my cheek. His dark hair pokes out from under his beanie, his cheeks and nose a rosy color from the cold air. The snow continues to fall around us and we're standing in the middle of the rink as others skate past us.

Asher's throat bobs as he stares down at me. His eyes shine back at me and his tongue darts out as he wets his lips. A shiver moves up my spine and it's not from the cold air of the winter night. My fingers dig into his shoulders as I hold on to him for dear life.

His face dips down to mine, his lips soft as he presses them to mine. Asher claims my mouth with his in a slow, gentle kiss. Instinctively, I wrap my arms around the back of his neck, pressing my body to his as his tongue tangles with mine.

He slowly moves his lips against mine before pulling away. His eyelids flutter open, bouncing back and forth between mine as he searches my eyes for any regret or hesitancy. Asher presses his lips to mine again before he puts some space between us.

"You want to get some hot chocolate and get you warmed up?"

I stare back at him for a moment, my chest rising and falling with every shallow breath that escapes me. He caught me off guard, throwing me off-balance with the kiss. And then he goes and acts like it didn't just happen. He's giving me whiplash and I'm not sure if he knows what he's doing.

Because friends don't kiss friends the way he just kissed me.

CHAPTER THIRTEEN
ASHER

"Did you guys have a good time?" my mother asks us as Sydney and I walk into the kitchen. It's already well into the evening and my father must have retired to bed for the night.

My mother and my two sisters are sitting at the dining room table, playing Scrabble as they all sip some wine. Catherine rises to her feet, grabbing a glass for Sydney before she motions for her to take the seat next to her.

Sydney takes the glass from Catherine and thanks her as she walks over to the seat that is pulled out for her. I watch her for a moment as she takes off her coat and hat before sitting down. "It was lovely," she tells my mother, offering her a warm smile. "I had never been ice skating before, so it was a little nerve-racking."

A soft chuckle falls from my lips as I drop down into the seat next to Sydney. Catherine gives me a glass of wine, but I don't touch it as I let it sit in front of me on the table. "She was a little shaky at first, but she got it."

"Yeah, right," she snorts before taking a sip from her glass. "If there's one thing I will never be able to do, it's skate like you do."

My mother laughs lightly. "I don't know if any of us would ever be able to do that. Not when he's been skating basically since he could walk."

"Were you and your husband the ones who got Asher into ice hockey?" Sydney asks my mother, glancing at me from the corner of her eye.

"My husband always enjoyed hockey, but that poor man doesn't have an athletic bone in his body." My mother laughs, looking up at me. "He was watching hockey one day when Asher was little and he fell in love with the sport as soon as he saw it. Living in Maine, everyone pretty much learns how to ice skate at a young age, but we got him into hockey as soon as he expressed his interest in it and never looked back."

My mother looks over at me, with nothing but

pride shining in her eyes as she stares at me. A smile tugs on the corners of her lips and Lucy makes a gagging sound from her seat next to our mom.

"We get it, Mom." Lucy rolls her eyes as Catherine bats at her. "Asher is your favorite and always will be. Can we for once not talk about him and damn hockey?"

I look at my sister for a moment, feeling her words like a slap to the face. Lucy is the second oldest and she's always been the one who was bitter about me playing hockey. I think in a way she felt like she was forgotten, but she was the only one out of all of us that didn't get involved in any sports or activities. Our parents put as much time and dedication into each kid and the sport we played. It wasn't my fault Lucy spent most of her time out partying instead.

Sydney looks over at me, her eyes widening slightly as she awkwardly shifts her weight in her seat. Her cheeks are still a pink color from the cold air when we went skating. I shouldn't have kissed her, but I was so caught up in the moment, it happened before I had the chance to stop it.

Neither of us spoke a word about the moment we shared and I don't know that we should. She let me buy her hot chocolate after we were done on the ice and it was as if everything was back to normal. Except for the tension that hung heavily in the air between us. It was suffocating, and I know the only way to make it stop is by having a conversation with her.

The very conversation that I refuse to have.

I can't discuss my feelings with her, not when I'm trying my hardest to ignore them at all costs. Sydney might be one of my closest friends, but she has her own life and I'm not going to disrupt that. I have had dreams of the NHL after college since I was a kid. I can't get involved with someone else and force them into a demanding life like that.

Even if I want Sydney in my life.

I want more with her and I know that now. But it can never happen. I don't know what her plans are after graduation but I can't ask her to sacrifice any of that to live the life as someone who is dating a hockey player. It just wouldn't work and I would never forgive myself if I made her feel like she had to give something up.

Sydney has her own dreams and I refuse to be the one who comes between her achieving them.

Even if it hurts my heart in the process.

My mother and my sisters finish their game of Scrabble and glasses of wine before they begin to make their way to their respective bedrooms. My sisters are the first to go, both of them finding their husbands in the den watching TV before they head off to sleep. My mother is the last to go, and she stops by Sydney before she disappears from the room.

"Thank you for going skating with him. It's something we all usually do every year, but I've been really struggling with my cold intolerance, so I wasn't feeling well enough to go this time."

Sydney stares back at her for a moment, her eyes filled with sympathy as she nods. "It was my pleasure. As annoying as Asher can be, I enjoy spending time with him."

My mother laughs lightly, pulling Sydney in for a quick hug before coming over to me. Sydney finishes her glass of wine and takes it over to the sink as my mother pulls me in for a hug. "I like her," she whispers as she pulls away from me. Her eyes bounce back and forth between mine. "I can tell she makes you happy and that makes me happy too."

I smile back at my mother, feeling the words getting caught in my throat. She isn't wrong, Sydney does make me happy. She reminds me that there's more to life than the sport I've dedicated all of my time to. And that she's someone who is worth spending my time with instead of worrying about other shit.

It hurts a little that I can't tell my mom the truth. I hate that I'm deceiving her in this moment, making her believe this is really real between the two of us. I can tell how much she enjoys Sydney and I hate that I'm going to have to break it to her eventually. She'll never have to know that all of this was fake, but there's going to come a time where she's going to know that Sydney and I aren't together.

My mother retires to her bedroom for the night and Sydney strolls back over to me. She stops for a moment, tilting her head to the side as she raises an eyebrow at me.

"Is everything okay?" she questions me, her eyes bouncing back and forth between mine as she searches for something that could be amiss.

Recovering from the sadness that momentarily clouded my brain, I offer her a smile and shake my head. "It's nothing. I'm good."

Sydney stares at me for a moment, her eyes suspicious as she doesn't buy me dismissing her, but she doesn't press the issue. I'm half waiting for her to question me on it more or to call me out on my bullshit, but she doesn't.

And I'm wondering if she's afraid to know what was really on my mind in that moment.

"Are you ready to go to bed?" she asks, her voice soft as she nervously shifts her weight on her feet. "I'm pretty exhausted from tonight and if I remember correctly, we're going to the gardens to see the Christmas lights tomorrow, right?"

A smile touches my lips and I nod. "We have these little Christmas traditions that we usually do as a family."

"I love it." She smiles back at me. "My family never had traditions like that and it just shows how close your family really is. That there's more to Christmas than materialistic things. You are all together because you want to spend the time with one another. It's a nice reminder of what is actually important during the holidays."

I feel a crack in my armor, my heart splintering slightly at the sadness in Sydney's tone. With how humble and down to earth she is, it's easy to forget the affluent lifestyle she comes from. And it hurts my heart to think about her not having these same traditions. It's almost as if her family doesn't view one another as anything of importance.

"I'm really glad you are here with me," I tell her with nothing but honesty. "I know it was a lot to ask you to come to my brother's wedding, but I'm glad you came. And that you're going to be here for Christmas too."

Sydney smiles back up at me. "Me too," she whispers, her eyes shining back at me. The scent of her floral perfume invades my senses and I want to feel her warmth against me. I want her soft lips against mine.

But I can't do that to her.

I need to put some distance between us before I make a fucking mistake.

CHAPTER FOURTEEN
SYDNEY

Asher left earlier this morning to go shopping with his father. He made sure we both went downstairs and joined the rest of the family for breakfast before they left the house. His sisters and their husbands went to go visit some of their friends and his mother was going to go have lunch with one of her friends.

Before Asher left, he had invited me along but he was being weird about it. Almost as if he didn't actually want me to go but was extending the invitation just so things wouldn't be awkward. I didn't mind staying at their house by myself, but his behavior was weird and had me questioning everything.

Last night, he told me he was glad I came here and was staying with his family. And then instead of sleeping with me in bed again, he made a bed for himself on the floor. I didn't push the issue because I'm confused with everything that involves Asher right now. I can't get a read on him, and his words and actions aren't exactly matching up.

He was fine at breakfast, engaging in conversation and back to his normal self, but then when it was time for them to leave, there was a weird shift. He's giving me whiplash and honestly, it's getting a little exhausting. I'm okay if he just wants to be friends and go back to the way things were before the wedding.

But if we're going to do that, then we need to agree on some ground rules.

The first one being that he doesn't kiss me the way he did again.

With it being the dead of winter and frigid outside, I spend the day inside, laying in Asher's bed as I binge-watch some shows on Netflix. It's hard to not let my mind drift to him and the intimate moments we've shared, but I try my hardest to keep them from clouding my thoughts.

It's later in the afternoon when I hear Asher and his father arrive back home. He doesn't come up to his room for a little bit and I'm half tempted to go see what he's up to before I decide against it. After this morning, I'm not sure if I feel comfortable approaching him or not. Instead, I'll wait for him to come to me.

Sitting up in Asher's bed, I pull the blanket over my lap and prop myself up with some pillows as he enters the room. My eyes meet his and he flashes his straight white teeth at me as he sees that I've made myself at home in his bed.

"Sorry we were gone so long," he tells me as he walks over to the bed and drops down on the edge of it. "My father decided to wait until the last minute to buy everyone's presents."

"That's okay," I tell him as I pause the show I'm watching. The way he acted this morning is still on my mind, bothering me. "Can I ask you something?"

"Of course," he responds without hesitation as he turns to face me on the bed.

Pulling my lips between my teeth, I bite down on my bottom one before releasing it. "You were acting kind of weird this morning. Did I do something wrong? I obviously didn't want to impose on you and your father having the day out together, but you just seemed off before you left."

He stares at me for a moment, tilting his head to

the side as a worried look passes through his eyes. "I wasn't trying to act weird at all. I'm sorry if I made it seem like I was being off or something. I wanted you to come along, but I didn't want you to because I have a surprise. And I'm trying really hard to not spoil it."

"What kind of a surprise?" I question him, my eyebrows pulling together. Suddenly, it dawns on me why he didn't want me to come shopping with them. "Asher, I swear... you better not have bought me a Christmas gift."

Asher smiles brightly at me and my stomach sinks. I didn't have the chance to buy him anything and the last thing I need is for him to get me a gift. That is one of the worst feelings in the world for me. I hate when someone gets me something and I don't have anything to give them in return.

"Don't worry about it." He laughs lightly as he kicks off his shoes and climbs farther onto the bed. I move over enough to give him some room as he slides under the covers and props his head on a pillow. "Tell me about your day. And what show I'm about to get sucked into with you."

I tell Asher the extent of my day and how I've essentially been in the same place since after breakfast. He seems content, knowing that I spent the day relaxing without any worries. Little does he know, I struggled with thoughts of him all damn day long. He seems interested in the show as soon as I tell him about it and we fall into a comfortable silence as he grabs the remote and presses Play.

There's a part of me that wants to push the issue of him potentially buying me a Christmas gift, but for now, I'll let it go. I just need to find some way to sneak away and get him a gift too. With Christmas Eve being tomorrow night, I don't know how I'm going to get away. Perhaps I can borrow his mom sometime tomorrow and she can take me out.

I hate the thought of having to ask anyone for favors while I'm here. They've already taken me in as if I'm a part of their family and I hate asking for any more than they've already given me. But I'm kind of limited with my options here, especially since I came with Asher and he's my only resource to get around town.

Not to mention the fact that I have no idea where anything is around here anyway. This is a brand-new place that I've never been to and I don't know where the closest shopping mall even is.

We watch two more episodes of the show I've

immersed myself in and Asher is completely on board with it. That's one of the things I love about him and our friendship. We get along so well and everything is just so damn easy between us. I can't let what happened between us ruin this at all. I need to separate my feelings for him and just let things resume how they were before we came here.

Asher's mother comes to the bedroom door, knocking lightly on it before he tells her to come in. She gently pushes open the door, a smile on her face as she sees the two of us watching TV together.

"Were the two of you ready to go to the gardens soon?" she asks as she hovers in the doorway. "Your father and I were talking about us all getting dinner before going."

"That sounds perfect," Asher tells her, returning her smile as he sits up in bed and throws off the covers. "When did you want to head out?"

His mother looks over to me. "How long do you need to get ready, Sydney?"

"Probably only fifteen minutes," I respond, shrugging lightly. I took a shower this morning after everyone left so I just need to throw on some makeup and some real clothes.

"Perfect," she smiles, her eyes bouncing back and forth between the two of us. "We were thinking about driving separately. Just in case it gets too cold and your father and I decide to leave early."

"Whatever you want to do is good with us," Asher rises to his feet as he walks over to his dresser and pulls out a pair of jeans. "I don't want you to be uncomfortable out there, so driving separately is perfectly fine."

Rachel nods, her smile falling slightly as a wave of sadness passes through her eyes. I know that her doctors are hoping they can safely declare that she's in remission now, but it's clear she's still physically struggling from everything her body went through. And it breaks my heart for her.

"I'll see you guys downstairs in a little bit," his mother tells us before she disappears from his room, pulling the door shut behind her.

Asher strips out of his sweatpants and my eyes widen as I watch him from where I'm still sitting in his bed. I know I've already seen him naked, but this feels like I should be giving him some privacy.

"I'll leave the room so you can get changed," I tell him, nervousness lingering in my words as I quickly climb out of his bed. My legs get tangled in the blankets and I practically fall onto the floor.

Laughter rumbles from Asher's chest and he raises an eyebrow at me as I get up from the floor.

"Babe, you've already seen me naked. I'm just changing into a pair of jeans and a hoodie. It's nothing you haven't seen already."

I swallow hard over the lump in my throat, feeling the warmth creep up my neck and rapidly spread across my cheeks. Turning my back to him, I walk over to where my suitcase is and grab a change of clothes from it. As I turn back around to face him, Asher is standing there with his watchful gaze on me.

We've already crossed a line and there's no coming back from that. I shouldn't play with his head, but he's been giving me whiplash, so it's only right I give him a taste of his own medicine.

My eyes meet his and I challenge him with a hard stare as I pull my shirt over my head. His gaze trails over my breasts that are covered by my bra and I watch his throat bob. Sliding my fingers under the waistband of my pajama pants, I push them down my thighs until I'm standing in front of him in just my underwear and bra.

Asher's irises ignite as a fire burns in his gaze. He doesn't tear his eyes away from me as I stare him down. I know I'm pushing the limits of our friendship, which is a complete contradiction to wanting to preserve it instead of ruin it. But Asher has been toying with me, going back and forth with him putting distance between us and then kissing or touching me.

Two can play this game...

But I'm afraid neither of us will win.

CHAPTER FIFTEEN
ASHER

Sydney is fucking with my head, with the way she practically stripped in front of me, knowing I couldn't touch her in that moment. I don't know what the hell we're doing here and I don't even know if I want to stop it at this point.

I don't want to ruin our friendship, but in this moment, I'm so close to saying fuck it all.

Let's completely obliterate our friendship and see where the hell this goes.

Dinner is fairly mundane, and that's to be expected with my family. It feels like the time we spend in the restaurant drags on, especially with Sydney sitting next to me in the booth—her warm thigh pressed against mine the entire time.

I want to take her home and throw her on my bed instead of bothering to go look at the Christmas lights. She's working her way under my skin and I don't know if I can possibly shake this feeling she's brought to life inside me. I've never wanted a relationship before, but I can't seem to get this damn girl out of my head.

As badly as I want to take her home, I know I can't do that. This is a family tradition we do every single Christmas and one that we've been doing since we were all kids. We tried to do it last year, but my mother didn't last long. She was undergoing her treatment at the time and tried so hard to push through.

She ended up being completely exhausted after only twenty minutes of walking around so we called it quits and went home and watched Christmas movies instead. I could tell at the time that it was breaking her heart. She felt like she was letting us all down and ruining the tradition that we had been doing for years.

And this year, she finally feels up to it. Even if she doesn't make it the entire time we're here, this still means the world to her. And my mother is the one person in my life that I will do everything in my power to avoid disappointing.

So, taking Sydney back to my room will have to wait. And I don't even know if that's a smart move. With the feelings she's brought out in me, I know it's only a matter of time before it happens again. Before we go back to campus, I will have her again. Even if it's only one last time. I had a small taste of her and it wasn't enough for me.

We all head to the gardens in our separate cars, Sydney riding with me. She doesn't bring up her little charade of stripping for me earlier. Instead, she's cheerful and chatty, talking about how wonderful her time has been with my family. And I would be lying if I said it didn't make my heart swell.

Even though she's had a good life with her parents in a financial and materialistic way, she deserves so much more than they ever gave her. And I'm happy to be the one who gets to show her the better parts of life. The important things that will always remain in your mind as a memory, but there are ones that are much more impactful than a Louis Vuitton bag or a pair of Louboutins.

We arrive at the gardens and meet the rest of my family out front. We all head in together and I watch Sydney in awe as her eyes light up at the Christmas tree display at the front entrance. My parents already paid for our tickets in advance, so we all go through the entrance without a hitch.

My sisters walk with their husbands and my father and mother walk behind the four of them, hand in hand. That's one thing I love about them; the only thing that has given me a small piece of hope for when I eventually settle down. They've been married for thirty years and are still in love like when they first started dating.

If I ever do get married, I want a love like what they have.

Sydney walks along beside me, her eyes wide in wonderment as she takes in all of the different displays of Christmas lights. Judging by the look on her face and the different things she's told me about her childhood, I don't think she's ever seen anything like this before.

I can't help myself as I reach out for her, wrapping my hand around hers. Her palm is warm through her glove as she presses it to mine, lacing our fingers together. She glances at me, her eyes finding mine as a smile plays on her lips.

I love the way she looks right now, bundled up in her puffy winter coat. A white scarf is wrapped around her neck, her long hair spilling down her back with a beanie covering the top of her head.

She's a California girl, but she looks like she belongs in my world.

Lost in a winter wonderland together.

Neither of us say a word as we walk hand in hand through a tunnel of lights. They shift, changing colors to the beat of the holiday music that plays in the background. The entire place is fucking magical and I have no shame whatsoever saying that.

I love being able to share this with Sydney. The different displays of Christmas trees and lights is an experience in itself. We walk through the gardens, separating from my family as they all stop to get some hot chocolate.

Sydney said she didn't want any and instead wanted to explore the maze of hedges that they have here. All of the bushes are covered with different lights and as we walk through, we find small displays throughout. As we reach the center of the maze, there's a massive Christmas tree with a sparkling star on the top of it.

"This entire place is amazing," Sydney says softly as we stand by the tree, both of our heads tilted back as we stare at the twinkling lights. "I've never experienced something like this. Like, nowhere close to this at all. Thank you so much for sharing this with me."

I want to share more than just Christmas with you.

"I'm really glad to be the one to show you all of this," I tell her with nothing but honesty as I turn to look at her. "Knowing that I get to be here with you has honestly made this holiday the best one I've had in a long time."

Sydney smiles up at me, a shyness creeping over her expression that makes my heart melt. She's feisty at times and has no problem calling me on my bullshit, but I love this innocent side of her too. Even though we've been friends for three years, the shift between us has her acting like she's shy around me from time to time.

And there's a part of me that loves this newness between us.

I can't let my mind go there, though... I can't entertain thoughts of anything other than friendship between us. Just because her hand is in mine right now doesn't mean a damn thing. We're here with my family, and she's just simply playing the part I asked her to play.

Too bad I'm tired of playing this charade...

CHAPTER SIXTEEN
SYDNEY

"Good morning, Sydney," Rachel, Asher's mom greets me the next morning as I walk into the kitchen. She's busying herself over the stove, cooking breakfast for everyone. She motions to the coffee pot and mugs. "Help yourself if you'd like some coffee."

Smiling at her, I walk over and pour myself some before mixing in some creamer. I glance out the back windows, watching Asher as he stands out in the middle of the snow-covered yard. My head tilts to the side out of confusion as I watch him with a perplexed look on my face.

"What is he doing out there?" I question Rachel as I watch Asher's lips moving like he's talking to someone, but he's staring up at the roof instead.

"He's helping his father." She glances out where I'm looking, a soft laugh falling from her lips at how Asher looks like he's just talking to himself. "He's up on the roof, fixing some of the Christmas lights. That is who Asher is talking to."

"I thought maybe he was having a minor mental breakdown or something, out there staring at the sky as he talks to himself," I tell her, laughing along with her at how ridiculous the notion sounds now. When we got back here last night, he took to his bed on the floor again. He didn't cross the line any further while we were at the gardens. He didn't make an attempt to touch me or kiss me, other than holding my hand the entire night.

Perhaps he's decided it's best we keep things the way they are, putting on a show in front of everyone, and then we can resume to the way things were before.

Rachel finishes up at the stove and moves all of the food onto the table before calling up for Asher's sisters and their husbands to come eat. As I take my seat at the table, I glance over at Rachel who sits across from me.

"I have a favor to ask you, if that's okay?" I say, my voice quiet as I look over my shoulder at Asher still standing in the yard. "I was wondering if you could give me some ideas of what to get Asher as a gift."

A smile touches his mother's lips and she nods. "I have a few ideas. Did you want me to take you shopping today? I know you don't have a car or anything, and I don't think you really want to go shopping with him when he's who you're buying a gift for."

"That would be amazing." I smile back at her, feeling at ease with her warmth. "We never discussed gifts or anything like that and I'm pretty sure he got me something yesterday. I can't be the one who doesn't have something to give him in return."

Rachel looks at me for a moment. "Sweetie, you don't need to give that boy a gift. You being with him is more than enough. I don't know the last time I've seen him so happy about something that doesn't involve a stick or a puck."

I stare back at her, my eyes widening slightly as my lips part. Words fail me in this moment and thankfully, the rest of the family comes strolling into the dining room, effectively saving me from coming up with any type of a response to her admission.

———

Asher's mom takes me shopping, after telling them we were going out to get lunch. Asher didn't question it and instead seemed pleased that I was spending some time with his mother. She helped me pick out the perfect gift for him and I was able to sneak away to get everyone else something too. It only felt right, almost a way of showing my gratitude for them taking me in for the holiday.

There's a part of me that feels like I'm being no different than my parents. Their love language was always buying someone's love. They were never actually affectionate with me as a child and instead just spoiled me with materialistic things. I know that Asher's family doesn't need any types of gifts, but it's the only way I know how to show something other than just giving them my words.

Rachel takes Asher's gift from me as we pull into the driveway, promising me that she'll wrap it. It makes things much easier because I don't know when I'll have any time to sneak away from him and wrap it myself.

I grab my few bags of what I bought for everyone else and disappear up to Asher's bedroom when we get back to the house. It's Christmas Eve, and like the rest of the days, this evening is filled with another tradition. Thankfully, it's much more low-key than the rest of the activities that we've done. And with the way that the snow is beginning to fall outside, it seems like a good night to stay in.

"Hey you," Asher greets me softly from his bed as I walk into his room and softly shut the door behind me. He's watching some sports show, but he quickly mutes the TV and gives me all of his attention. "I was beginning to think maybe my mother kidnapped you or something. You guys were gone for a long time."

Rolling my eyes, I drop my bags onto his bed as I laugh at him. "We weren't gone that long. And I wanted to get your sisters and parents something for Christmas."

Asher sits up straighter in bed, his eyebrows tugging together. "You didn't have to get anyone anything."

"I know," I tell him as I drop down onto the edge of the mattress. "It just felt kind of weird thinking about being here with everyone tomorrow morning and not having a present to give anyone. It's nothing big, it's just small stuff. Something to show my appreciation for them extending their home to me for the holiday."

His head tilts to the side, a thoughtful look passing through his eyes and a smile creeps across his mouth. "I'm pretty sure my mom is just glad to see me bring someone home for once."

His words sink in, a sadness washing over me as reality rears her ugly head. It's been so easy to get caught up in this alternate reality that sometimes it slips my mind that none of this is actually real. I've been spending time with his family and after Christmas, I don't know if I'll ever see them again.

"What's wrong?" Asher questions me, his voice worried as his smile falls from his face.

"Nothing," I tell him dismissively, shaking my head. "I have just really enjoyed my time here with you and your family. Dare I say, this might be the best Christmas I've ever had."

Asher stares at me for a moment. "So, why do you seem upset about that?"

I swallow hard over the lump lodged in my throat. "Because I know this will never happen again."

My words hang heavily in the air between us and Asher's eyes don't leave mine. I watch his throat as it bobs while he swallows. His lips part slightly, like he wants to say something, but he quickly clamps them back together. A sigh slips from my lips as I turn away from him, casting my gaze down to my hands in my lap.

The mattress dips, shifting under Asher's weight as he moves across the bed. My breath catches in my throat as I feel his warmth. He positions himself behind me, my back pressed to his warm chest as he wraps his arms around the front of my body.

"It doesn't have to be like that," he whispers, his lips brushing against the shell of my ear. A shiver goes directly up my spine. His words soothe my soul, but I don't know what he means by that.

I don't bother asking him, both of us falling silent as he presses his lips to my neck. They're soft and warm against my skin and I instantly relax against him. I'm afraid to ask what he might have meant by his words and he doesn't bother to elaborate... almost as if he's afraid to.

"Do you want to get these presents wrapped? Or we can do it later?"

"Aren't we supposed to be doing something later?"

Asher chuckles lightly, burying his head in the crook of my neck. "On Christmas Eve, we usually watch Hallmark movies together and eat the millions of cookies that my mom made." He pauses for a moment, lifting his head as he rests his chin against my shoulder. "And don't you dare tell anyone that I watch any of those movies, you got it?"

Laughter bubbles from my chest and I shake my head. "You afraid to have anyone know that you actually have a soft side and some feelings?"

"Exactly," he murmurs. I instantly feel his absence as he moves away from me, a rush of cold air replacing his warmth against my back. "Let's wrap them now so we don't have to worry about it after everyone goes to bed."

It's almost as if the moment between us never happened, but Asher doesn't act any differently toward me. He's back to his normal self as he slips out of the room before returning with some wrapping paper, scissors, and tape. He sits cross-legged on the floor by the bed, spreading everything out as I grab my bags and sit down on the floor with him.

By the time we're finished, it's time to head downstairs for dinner. His mother ordered pizza, since I would imagine she's tired of having to cook for so many people. Especially with all of the cooking that will be done tomorrow.

After everyone eats, we all settle in the living room with popcorn and cookies and Christmas Hallmark movies. Asher pulls me down onto the couch beside him, wrapping his arm around my shoulders as he moves me flush against him. I glance up at him for a moment, no one paying any attention to us.

"I don't think we need to convince them any more that we're together," I whisper to him, feeling too comfortable with how his arm feels around me. I need to separate myself from him in an attempt to get him out of my head. My thoughts are too cloudy when it comes to him, and I'm almost beginning to believe this is real too.

"Who said that I'm trying to convince anyone anymore?" he murmurs, his eyes shining back at me as a ghost of a smile plays on his lips. "Now, be quiet. The movie is about to start and this is one of my favorites."

A giggle slips from my lips and I lean closer, nestling in against him as everyone else piles onto the couch to watch the movie. I'll worry about sifting through my muddled thoughts when all of this is over.

For now, I'm going to enjoy the time I have with him, even if it's going to hurt me in the end.

CHAPTER SEVENTEEN
ASHER

Last night, Sydney ended up falling asleep on the couch while we watched movies and I couldn't bring myself to wake her up. Instead, I stayed where I was and fell asleep sitting up after covering her with a blanket, letting her use me as a pillow. At some point we must have shifted, because when I woke up this morning, we were spooning on the couch.

Sydney's chest rises and falls with every breath she takes and I wrap my arm tighter around her, reveling in the feeling of her this close. We have to go back to Vermont tomorrow... back to reality, where she isn't my girlfriend anymore.

Honestly, I would love to stay in this alternate reality for a little longer.

The aroma from the food that my mother is cooking invades my senses. Sydney stirs in my arms as a loud sound comes from the kitchen. The house is already coming to life as everyone makes their way back into the living room.

Sydney is awake now, but she lays silently for a moment, almost as if she doesn't want this moment to end either.

"Asher?" she says softly, her voice quiet as she continues to lay in my arms. "Are you awake?"

"I am," I tell her, not loosening my grip around her waist. "How did you sleep?"

"Considering the fact that we slept on the couch, pretty well," she laughs lightly. "Sorry I fell asleep during the movie. I must have been pretty tired."

"Don't apologize, Syd." I pause for a moment, carefully choosing my words before deciding fuck it. "I enjoyed sleeping down here with you."

She's silent again for a moment, before she begins to shift in my arms. "I really need to go to the bathroom. And it sounds like everyone's already awake."

Moving my arm away from her, I give her space to get up and she quickly climbs to her feet. "I'm just going to go to the bathroom quick and brush my teeth and stuff."

I offer her a small smile, but it doesn't feel like it comes anywhere close to reaching my eyes. "I'll meet you back in here."

Sydney smiles at me, looking nervous before she disappears from the room. I hear the door shut to the downstairs bathroom and I climb off the couch, heading back upstairs. I slip into the bathroom on the second floor and relieve my bladder before brushing my teeth. As I finish up and leave the room, Sydney is there, waiting to go inside to brush her teeth.

Neither of us say a word as I slide past her and head up into my bedroom. I don't know why there's a weirdness between us suddenly. I think the heaviness of tomorrow is weighing on both of us and I need to figure out how I can get more time with Sydney.

I'm not ready for this to be over.

Grabbing the presents that we wrapped last night, I head downstairs to meet up with everyone in the living room. Everyone is already down there except for Sydney. My mother is passing out the gifts to everyone and I take a seat in front of the small pile that has ones labeled with my name. There's a small pile beside mine, all with Sydney's name on them.

It warms my heart, the way my family has just

taken her in like she's always been a part of our family. And that just solidifies the decision I know I need to make. I want more of her time; I want all of her. And right now, there's only two ways this is going to go.

All or nothing.

Our friendship is already ruined and there's no way either of us can go back to the way things were before. So, we're left with no choice. Either she's a part of my future or I have to let her go completely. Because after spending this time together, I don't know that I can have her in my life if she doesn't want more with me.

Sydney appears in the doorway, her eyes meeting mine before she walks over and sits down on the plush rug beside me. Her eyes widen as she sees the presents that my mother set out for her, all labeled from my family members. "What is this?" She looks up at me, her eyes wet with emotion.

"Exactly what it looks like." I wink at her. "They're pretty fucking smitten by you."

She swallows hard as she recovers from the emotion that threatened to consume her. Reaching past me, she begins to pick up the presents that she got everyone and passes them around the circle. Everyone seems surprised that she got them something, since it was never a requirement for her being here.

I never expected Sydney to get anyone anything and she surprised me when she did. She was sneaky, having my mom take her out. I don't know how she managed to pull off getting everyone something with my mother hovering around, but somehow she did.

She got each of my sisters and my mother a necklace. They're all delicate, with small diamonds encrusted in the swirled design. I don't pay any attention to what she gets either of my brothers-in-law or father as she hands me a small box.

"You didn't have to get me anything, babe," I tell her, my voice soft as her eyes search mine. I watch as a pink tint spreads across her cheeks and she ducks her head slightly. "But first, open mine," I tell her, as I reach behind my back and grab two boxes for her.

Sydney takes them from me, her eyes widening as she stares at me for a moment. "What the hell, Ash," she mumbles, shaking her head. "First, we never agreed on gifts. And now you went and got me two instead?"

"Shhh," I shush her, pressing my finger against her soft plump lips. "Just shut up and open them."

Sydney starts with the bigger box, pulling off the

wrapping paper before she reaches the box underneath. She takes off the lid, my stomach doing flips as I watch her face light up. Reaching inside, she grabs the yoke of the shirt and lifts it up, holding it in the air.

"You got me a jersey?" she questions me, staring at the black Wyncote Wolves jersey. I watch her as she turns it to see the back, noting the number 30 and Golding in bold white letters. "Oh my god, you got me one of your jerseys?"

I smile at her, feeling my heart swell at how genuinely happy she is about it. She's come to a few of my games before, but only as a friend. And never with one of my jerseys on. Hopefully we can change how that goes down in the future, and I can't wait to see her in it.

I don't tell her, but I had gotten the jersey for her before we even left to come here. I don't know what compelled me in the moment, but I can take a safe guess now that it had to do with my feelings for her that I was trying to bury deep inside.

"Open yours," she insists as she carefully folds the jersey and puts it back in the box.

My eyes meet hers and I shake my head. "Nope. You first and then I'll open mine."

Sydney rolls her eyes as a sigh slips from her

lips and she tears at the wrapping paper on the smaller box. She glances up at me, her throat bobbing as she notices that it's a black velvet box. My heart crawls into my throat as I watch her lift the lid, her eyes lighting up when she sees what is inside.

"Oh my god, Asher," she breathes, her voice barely audible over everyone else laughing in the background. Part of me forgot that my family was even present in the room as our surroundings seem to dissipate whenever Sydney is near me. "This is such a beautiful set."

I watch her as she plucks the diamond earrings from inside the box and slides them through the holes in her ears. She carefully takes the matching necklace out and looks at me, holding it out. "Will you help me put this on?"

"Of course," I tell her, my voice hoarse. I take the necklace from Sydney and she turns to face the opposite direction, showing me her back. Wrapping her hands around her long thick hair, she pulls it over her shoulder as I unclasp the necklace and loop it around her neck.

She grabs the diamond pendant with her other hand, holding it in place as I secure it around the back of her neck. My fingertips brush against her skin and my heart thumps as I feel her warmth beneath my fingers.

Sydney turns back around to face me, releasing her hair before she positions the necklace on her chest. "How does it look?"

"Fucking perfect," I breathe, staring deep into her eyes. "And I don't just mean the necklace."

Sydney stares back at me for a moment, her eyes glossing over as she swallows hard. Her lips part slightly, almost as if she's going to say something, but instead her tongue darts out as she wets them. "Open yours now."

A chuckle vibrates in my chest at her persistence and I oblige. Picking up the small box she had gotten me, I tear off the paper and open the box beneath it. I didn't pay attention to the name that was inscribed on the lid, but as I flip it open and see the watch inside, I'm at a loss for words.

This is too much. She couldn't have spent this much money on me.

"A Rolex?" I look up at her, shaking my head. "I can't accept this, Syd. This is way too much."

She purses her lips, tilting her head to the side. "Money doesn't matter, Asher. It's a nice watch and I thought you would like it. If you don't like it, I can take it back and you can pick something else out."

"No, that's not it at all. It's fucking awesome, but I can't accept something this expensive."

"Can you forget about how much it may have cost and maybe just think of it as a nice gift?"

There's a weird tension between us and I'm not sure who is more uncomfortable in this moment. My family doesn't come from money like hers does, so it feels weird accepting a gift like this. Especially when the necklace and earrings I got her are only a fraction of how much this watch cost.

"I'm sorry," I tell her, my eyes desperately searching hers. "I didn't mean to offend you. I just know this was probably really expensive and I didn't spend near as much on you."

"Asher, we don't live in the 1950s... a woman is allowed to spend more on a man."

My sisters both choke out a laugh, as they must have caught the tail end of our conversation. I slice my eyes to them, but the sound of my mother clearing her throat grabs my attention. As I glance over at her, she gives me a look of disapproval, and I suddenly feel guilty for the whole thing.

"We still have some time before dinner is ready, so who wants to watch some more Hallmark movies and play some board games?" my mother asks, trying to clear the awkwardness in the air.

It doesn't quite erase the tension between the two of us, but as I rise to my feet and hold my hand out to Sydney, she slides her palm against mine without any hesitation. I lift her to her feet and she doesn't let go of me as we all head to the couch to settle in for a movie.

I want to enjoy the rest of my time with her, because tomorrow is our last day here. And then will come the day that will come down to the choice we have to make. I'm going to leave the ball in Sydney's court, but I have no idea how she's going to react to it.

And I've never dreaded anything more.

CHAPTER EIGHTEEN
SYDNEY

The past five days have flown by. I was nervous coming here and having to meet Asher's family, and now I'm hating the thought of having to leave here tomorrow. This is our last day in Maine and thinking about going home has my stomach in knots.

I loved every minute I've been here and I don't know what Asher has planned for us, since it's our last day. His sisters and their husbands left this morning after breakfast, so it's just been the two of us and Asher's parents here.

His mother seems pretty exhausted after the holidays and even though I know she hates having her children leaving again, I think she's happy to have some quiet here again. Asher's sisters don't live far away so she will still see them frequently. Asher, on the other hand—with him living in a different state—it seems like there's a sadness that has crept in when she talks to him about our journey home tomorrow.

"You know, there's a part of me that wishes I didn't have to go back," Asher admits quietly as we sit in the den by the fireplace. We're both on the couch together, although there's some space between us as we both watch the flames crackle over the burning logs.

"You don't like Vermont?"

Asher looks over at me and shrugs. "I do, but it's not the same as being home. Don't get me wrong, I love the guys and the team that I play on, but there's something about being around my family that I really miss when I'm not here."

"Do you feel like you've been more homesick since your mom's diagnosis last year?"

Asher nods. "I feel guilty as hell for not being around. I tried to be here as much as I could after she was first diagnosed, but it's not the same as living close to her. I'm glad my sisters are still nearby, so I know she isn't completely alone from her children, but I still feel fucking terrible about it."

He pauses for a moment, his eyes bouncing back

and forth between mine, before he looks back to the fire. "If something were to happen while I wasn't here, I don't know if I could ever forgive myself. And anything can literally happen to anyone at any given moment. I don't know... I know it's all unrealistic because if I make it to the NHL, I have no fucking clue where I'll be then." He pauses again as a frown forms on his lips. "I could end up on the other side of the country and I don't know what the hell I'd do then."

"You can always visit them, Asher," I tell him, my voice gentle as I try to comfort him in any way I can. "And I'm sure they wouldn't be opposed to coming to wherever you end up living too."

Asher looks back at me, an indistinguishable look in his eyes. "Will you come visit me wherever I am?"

My heart crawls into my throat. "Of course. All you have to do is call me and I'll be there."

He stares at me for a moment, his eyes staring directly into my goddamn soul. "What if I want you to be closer than a phone call away?"

A shiver tears up my spine from the way he's looking at me right now. My body feels like it's on fire and my eyes widen as I stare back at him, unable to produce any words.

"I'm not ready for this to be over, Sydney," he tells me, his voice soft, barely audible. "This whole fake relationship… I don't know if I can go back to the way things were before."

"What do you mean?"

"I know we didn't want to ruin our friendship, but I think we're already past that point." He pauses for a moment, taking a deep breath as his eyes desperately search mine. "I don't think I can just be your friend anymore. I can't go back to that."

My heart pounds erratically in its cage and I stare back at him, still speechless. A ragged breath falls from my lips as I attempt to recover from his admission. "What do you want then?"

"I want you," he breathes, holding nothing back. "I want all of you. Our time together wasn't enough for me and I know that might sound pretty fucking greedy, but I don't care. I can't keep pretending I don't have feelings for you, because I do."

This is what I've wanted from him for so long, even though I never wanted to ruin our friendship. Asher always made it clear that he doesn't do relationships and would never have any interest in that with anyone. It's a complete shift from what he's always led me to believe and now he's telling me how he's really feeling, I don't know how the hell to mentally process it.

This is what I've been waiting for... so why the hell am I questioning it now?

"You promised me," I whisper, my breath catching in my throat as my eyebrows tug together. "You promised you wouldn't fall in love with me."

Asher's throat bobs as he swallows hard. "I know I did, but I broke that fucking promise, Sydney, and I don't regret it one bit."

"We were supposed to just go back to the way things were before."

He tilts his head to the side, a wave of pain washing through his eyes. "Is that what you want?"

"I don't know..." I pause for a moment, my words hanging heavily in the air. "This was never supposed to happen. You promised me and said that this was just to appease your mother. You invited me here to be your fake girlfriend, and now you're asking for more."

Asher abruptly rises to his feet and the pain on his face shatters my heart. "I don't know what else to say, Sydney. I'm not going to lie to you. You deserve the truth, even if it isn't what either of us expected. I told you how I feel and now it's your choice what you want to do with that information."

He spins on his heel, striding out of the room without another word. I'm left alone, staring at the doorway he just walked through, with no fucking clue of what to do.

I've had feelings for Asher for a long time now, but I've kept them to myself and buried them deep inside. We crossed a line and muddied the waters and now we're both sinking. The future is so unpredictable and what scares me the most is what will happen after we graduate.

I'm left with a decision to make and because of my fear of having my heart broken, I don't know what to do.

Either I drown in the waters with him or I swim out alone.

CHAPTER NINETEEN
ASHER

Walking away from Sydney just now may have been the hardest thing that I've ever done. I spilled my heart to her and put it all on the line. There was nothing left I could say or do. The ball is quite literally in her court and where we go from here is entirely up to her.

It's all or nothing at this point. There's literally no other option left with the lines we've crossed with our friendship. I could never go back to being just friends with her. And the thought of being friends and seeing her with another guy is enough to drive me mad.

Ignoring the bed I had made on the floor in my room, I collapse on my actual mattress instead. I don't care. Everything is already fucked, so I'm at least going to be comfortable as I drown in my own thoughts.

To be honest, Sydney didn't react the way I expected. The connection between us—what we have—it's completely undeniable. And she's neither stupid nor is she blind. Scared, maybe, but I know she feels the same way I do.

I didn't expect her to come running into my arms like a scene out of a romance movie, but I thought she would at least give me more than an "I don't know". I know I sprung it on her in a way I probably shouldn't have and I broke the promise I made to her, but it was quite literally out of my control.

How the hell could I have stopped myself from falling in love with her when I was already falling from the start?

My bedroom is dark and the rest of the house is silent. The only light that is in my room is from the moon hanging in the night sky outside my window. I didn't bother closing my blinds or curtains, so it shines directly through the glass panes, casting its light across the room.

I left Sydney down in the den and I have no idea what she plans on doing. The thought of her sleeping down there on the couch alone irritates me, but what am I supposed to do? Go beg her to come up here and sleep, just for us to wake up in the morning and go our separate ways when we get back to Vermont?

Fuck that.

I don't know what the hell I'm supposed to do right now and I hate that more than anything. Maybe I should have just kept my mouth closed instead and not tell her how I feel. My mother has taught me a lot in the past year since she was diagnosed with cancer. And if there's one thing that really stuck with me, it's our mortality and how short life really is.

I'm done wasting moments and time. Sydney deserved to know the truth and what she decides to do with it is up to her. I handed her my heart and now she gets to choose whether she keeps it or smashes it into a million little pieces.

My door slowly pushes open and I glance over, noticing Sydney as she slips inside the room. She softly closes it behind her, but she stops in her place, standing across the room from me in silence for a moment. The tension between us is palpable, like you could reach out and pluck it out of the air.

I don't move from where I'm lying on my bed,

standing my ground with the entire situation. She's the one who came to me, so it's her turn to talk. I just don't know if I'm ready to hear what she has to say.

A ragged breath slips from her and her footsteps are quiet as she slowly makes her way over to the bed. She doesn't stop as she reaches me, the mattress slightly dipping under her weight as she climbs onto it with me. She's silent as she settles on top of the comforter with me, lowering her body down beside mine.

Instinctively, I put out my arm for her as she slides up against me, her body against my side and her head on my chest. Bending my elbow, I wrap my arm around her shoulders and hold her as we lie in silence. It's confusing me—fucking with my head— and I just need her to say something. *Anything.*

"Hi," she says softly, her voice like music to my ears. "I'm sorry for the way I responded downstairs. It took me by surprise and you caught me off guard."

Staring up at the ceiling, my heart pounds erratically in my chest as I hold her against me. "Did it really surprise you, though? Don't bullshit me, Syd. I know you feel it too."

"You're right," she breathes, wrapping her arm

around my waist. "I just didn't expect you to say anything about it. I wasn't ready to hear about your feelings because I wasn't ready to admit my own."

Turning my head, I look down at the top of hers. "Are you ready to now?"

Sydney lifts her head, tilting it back as her eyes meet mine. "Yes."

She moves away from me, sitting up in the bed as she crosses her legs and stares down at me. Following her, I sit up with her, putting some space between us as I face her. Sydney takes a deep breath and I catch the look in her eye from the moonlight shining through my window. She looks terrified, but there's something else there. Something that matches the strong feelings I have in my heart for her.

"I don't want to be your friend either, Asher," she whispers after a few moments of silence. "I haven't wanted to be your friend for a long time, but I was always too afraid to ruin our friendship and be rejected by you."

"I'm pretty positive we have completely obliterated our friendship." I chuckle softly as I stare at her through the light that has cast across the room.

Her eyes search mine. "I'm just afraid of the

future. Neither of us can predict what will happen and I don't know that I could possibly survive you breaking my heart."

Scooting closer to her on the bed, I reach out for her, cupping the side of her face as I desperately search her gaze. "I will never break your heart, Sydney." I pause for a moment, brushing a stray hair away from her face. "Listen... I don't do relationships—at all. So this is pretty fucking serious for me. This isn't just a temporary thing for me. If I commit, I'm yours forever."

"How could you possibly say that?" she questions me, her voice catching in her throat as her eyes widen. "We're still in college, barely even started our lives."

"I guess when you know, you just know."

"And what do you know?"

I swallow roughly. "That I'm madly fucking in love with you, Sydney Phillips. And I want you for the rest of my life."

Her eyes grow wet and she climbs into my lap, linking her arms around the back of my neck and her legs around my waist. I watch as a tear falls down her cheek, and I reach out to catch it with the pad of my thumb. A soft laugh falls from her lips as her eyes shine back at me.

"I've been in love with you for a long time, Asher Golding." Her face dips down to mine, her lips barely brushing against my own. "And I'll love you for the rest of my life."

CHAPTER TWENTY
SYDNEY

Asher slides his hands up my torso, not stopping until he's cupping the sides of my face. He claims my mouth with his as he drains the air from my lungs. I have no idea where our future will lead, but I'm willing to take the plunge with him. After all, you never know what will happen if you don't take the risk.

And Asher is most definitely worth the risk.

His tongue slides along the seam of my lips, parting them before he slips inside. His tongue slides along mine before tangling together. We're caught up in the moment, our own little dance as our mouths move together, melting into one. Asher kisses me deeper until my head is spinning and he leaves me breathless.

Abruptly pulling away, his eyes bounce back and forth between mine as he holds the sides of my face. "I need you, Sydney. So fucking badly."

"Then take what you need, Asher," I breathe, my chest rising and falling with each shallow breath I take. My head is swimming, my heart pounding, as he stares back at me like he's seeing me for the first time.

He releases the sides of my face and he slides his hands down my torso before wrapping his arms around my ass. He lifts up onto his knees, taking me with him as I wrap my legs around his waist. Asher spins us both around on the bed before he lowers me down onto the mattress.

What started out as slow and gentle—sweet and tender—quickly becomes a race to the finish line. Asher lifts me up, just far enough to slide my shirt up over my head before tossing it onto the floor. His hands reach around my back, unclasping my bra before he pulls it away from my body, fully exposing my breasts, and discards that as well.

Lying on my back, I stare up at him as he reaches behind his neck and grabs his shirt. He pulls it over his head and throws it with the other clothes discarded on the floor. The moonlight that shines through his bedroom window casts the perfect amount across his body and my eyes travel along the planes of his abdomen and chest.

Staring at Asher as he looks down at me on the bed, I'm still in shock that this is where we are right now. Fuck the friendship we tried so hard to preserve. I'm ready for more with him and to see where all of this goes.

"I just need to know one thing," Asher murmurs as he slides his fingers under the waistband of my sweatpants. He lifts his eyes to mine as he slowly begins to drag them down my thighs, pulling them past my calves and feet, before dropping them onto the floor.

"Anything," I breathe, my chest rising and falling with every rapid breath as it feels like he's stealing the oxygen from the room. His presence literally takes up everything and I'm entirely consumed by him.

Asher hooks his fingers underneath the waistband of my panties and repeats the same movements, pulling them down my legs until I'm completely naked. I feel completely exposed, his gaze cutting past my skin and deep into my soul.

"Are you mine, Sydney?"

I stare up at him. "Yes."

"I'm not talking about just in this moment," he

says softly, as he slips out of his own sweatpants and boxers and leaves them on the floor by his feet. "I want you to be my girl. I want the entire fucking world to know you're mine."

"Then tell them," I challenge him, sitting up as I reach for him. He meets me halfway, climbing onto the bed as he lightly pushes me back onto the bed. "I'm yours, Asher. You have my entire heart and soul."

A fire burns in his eyes as he spits into his hand and wraps it around his cock, using his own saliva as lube. He settles back between my legs, hovering above me. "Good," he murmurs as he slowly pushes his cock inside me. "Because you have every piece of me."

His mouth drops down to mine as he steals my breath away once again. Wrapping my legs and arms around him, I hold on to him tightly as he begins to shift his hips, working his way inside me. This feels exactly where he belongs and he's worked his way into my heart and soul. And I'm certain I never want him to leave.

Asher fills me to the brim, his cock deep inside me as he begins to move with me. He props himself up on his forearm as he slides his hand through my hair, gripping close to my scalp. His other hand slides down to my hip and his finger-tips dig into my skin as he pins me in place. A warmth spreads through me and it's from him... it's all about him.

Thrust after thrust, he dives deeper inside me and I feel like I could come apart at the seams. I love this connection between us, as if nothing else in the world matters. Everything around us just has a way of fading away and we're the only thing that matters. This love we have between us—the one we've ignored for far too long.

Only now we can't ignore it any longer. And it's time we both let it completely consume us.

Asher pulls away from me, still inside me as he grabs my thighs and pulls them up toward him. He positions himself on his knees with my legs flat against his chest, my feet hooking around the back of his neck. A mischievous grin tugs on the corners of his lips as he slides his hand around the front, reaching between us.

Planting his palm against my groin, his thumb finds my clit. He applies the perfect amount of pres-sure as he rolls his thumb over the small bundle of nerves. The feeling alone of him inside me while playing with me has my eyes rolling backward in my head. Wrapping one of his arms around my thigh, he lifts my ass in the air as he straightens his spine while still on his knees.

After a few more thrusts, he begins to really pound into me, his balls slapping against my ass as he continues to roll his thumb around my clit. He strokes my insides with his cock, hitting all the right places as he plays me with his fingers like a skilled pianist stroking the ivory keys.

A warmth begins to spread across the bottom of my stomach and I can feel my orgasm building with every thrust inside me. I don't know which is driving me crazier—his cock pounding into me or his thumb rolling around my clit. Either way, he's pushing me closer and closer to the edge and I don't know how much longer I'm going to be able to hold on.

"Goddamn, babe," he groans, thrusting into me again. "Your pussy is gripping me so fucking tightly right now."

"I'm close," I moan as he presses harder against my clit, rolling his thumb in a circular motion. "So fucking close."

Asher stares down at me, a fire burning in his hooded gaze as he doesn't slow the movements of his hips. "Come for me, Sydney," he orders, his voice hoarse and thick with need. "Come all over my cock."

A moan slips from my lips, my eyes rolling back in my head as my orgasm hits me like a fucking earthquake. It completely takes over my body, tearing through me as I shatter around his cock. He continues to thrust into me, still playing with my clit as my legs shake. I'm falling deep into the abyss of ecstasy and I'm not sure I'll ever resurface from this. I'm not sure I ever want to even if I could.

Asher isn't far behind me, thrusting into me once more with my name on his lips as he loses himself in me. He doesn't bother to pull out as he fills me with his cum. I'm still riding out my orgasm with every nerve in my body, feeling like it's on fire. Asher slows down, thrusting into me once more as he completely empties himself inside me.

He pulls his hand away from my clit, grabbing my thighs with both of his hands as he gently lowers my ass back onto the mattress. He slowly pulls out of me and I instantly feel his absence, even though I'm filled with his warmth. A lazy grin forms on his lips as he stares down at me for a moment before rising off the bed.

We're both breathless as he collapses onto the mattress beside me. Rolling onto my side, I face him, my gaze finding his. He reaches out, brushing a piece of hair away from my face, and tucks it behind my ear.

"I never want this to end," I whisper, feeling overcome with emotion as the new situation we're in hits me. I love Asher and the thought of the future still has me scared.

"This is just the beginning, beautiful," he murmurs, his eyes shining at me.

I stare back at him. "The beginning of what?"

Asher smiles back at me and his eyes are filled with nothing but love.

"Our forever."

EPILOGUE
ASHER

SIX MONTHS LATER

"What are your plans for the summer, man?" Logan asks me as he sits down on the bench just outside of campus.

Today was the last day of our junior year and it was officially summer break. Although, for those of us who play hockey, it doesn't really mean much. Even though the season is over, that doesn't mean our time on the ice is over.

It's pretty standard for everyone to enroll in some type of summer league or different camps so we don't lose any of our skills. I don't think it would be possible to completely lose them, but ice time is precious time and we can't afford to lose that. None of us can afford to have any of our skills become rusty. Especially with senior year coming up in a few months.

That's all we need, to get through that final year and then we can finally move on with our careers. All of us have been shooting for the NHL, but it's not a known fact that we will all make it there. I have no doubt in my mind that Logan will be one of the ones that do make it.

"I'm actually going back home to Maine for the summer," I tell him, glancing over at him as he raises an eyebrow at me. "I'm going to do a summer league at the rink by my parents' house."

"Damn, dude, I didn't think you would be leaving us for the entire summer."

Other than when my mom was sick, this will be the first time going home that I'll be staying there for a significant amount of time. And it will be the first time in the past three years that I'm not playing with the guys that have become like my family.

"I know," I shrug, attempting to dismiss him. "I think it will be good for me to go home and spend some time with my family again. You know, your mom followed you out here, so you still get to see yours all the time."

"Yeah, I know..." He pauses for a moment,

chewing on the inside of his cheek. "I know that she has Owen, but I'm afraid she might lose her mind if I end up getting drafted farther away from her."

A laugh rumbles in my chest. "Your mom will fly out every damn week to watch you play wherever you are."

"True," he laughs along with me. "What about Sydney? Does she know you're going back to Maine for the summer?"

"We talked about it a little, but every time I try to bring it up, she acts like it isn't actually happening and shuts me down."

Logan looks off in the distance, his face lighting up as he spots something. My gaze follows after his and I see Isla, his girlfriend, strolling toward us. Logan looks back at me. "Did you ask Sydney to go back to Maine with you?"

A frown pulls the corners of my lips down. "I tried to, but she wouldn't give me a chance to even ask."

"So, don't ask," Logan offers with a shrug. "That girl loves you and will follow you to the ends of the earth. Buy her a plane ticket and see what happens."

"What are the two of you gossiping about?" Isla questions us with a smirk on her face as she stops in front of Logan.

Logan rises to his feet, stepping into her space as he wraps his arms around her waist. "Asher's going to Maine for the summer and is too much of a pussy to ask Sydney to go with him."

"That's not true," I retort, narrowing my eyes at him. "She hasn't given me the chance to ask her."

"Because she's afraid," Isla offers, her voice soft and gentle. "Look, getting involved with guys like the two of you isn't easy. It makes the future seem precarious and unpredictable. Show her that you are serious about her and what you really want. And when she tries to shut you down on it, don't let her."

"I don't want to force her to come or make her feel like she's obligated."

Isla shakes her head at me. "She won't and I know you wouldn't do that to her." She pauses for a second, gazing at Logan before looking back at me. "Let it be her decision and respect whatever she chooses. Just let her know you want her to come with you and you're not asking just as a formality."

I mull over her words for a moment, staring off into the distance as the two of them share a passionate kiss. Isla is right and I'm glad for both of their advice. I've been afraid to push the issue with Sydney because I don't want to scare her off. I don't want her to feel like she has to give anything up for me. But I can understand her reservations and her fears.

She's already expressed being afraid of what will happen after graduation and I've assured her that it changes nothing between us. If we end up in different states because of our careers, the only thing that changes is the amount of distance and how often we see each other. It changes nothing about my feelings for her and how much I fucking love the girl.

Logan and Isla turn their attention back to me, saying bye before they disappear out to the parking lot. I know I will see Logan again before I leave for the summer, so them leaving abruptly isn't surprising. Plus, the two of them are attached at the hip and can barely keep their hands off one another.

I would rather them take that elsewhere, because I have something much more important to attend to. I need to go find my girl and convince her to come with me.

I don't bother calling Sydney before stopping at her place. She has a habit of going home directly after she's finished with her last class and nine times out of ten, I end up coming here at some point in the evening. It's nice, being able to show up unannounced and knowing she's expecting me anyway.

Using the key Sydney gave me, I let myself into her apartment. The soft sound from the TV comes from the living room, but she's nowhere to be found when I walk into the room. As I walk through her apartment and head down the hallway, I see light shining from under the crack of her bathroom door.

Inching closer, I hear the sound of the shower running. Grabbing the handle, it's unlocked as I turn it and let myself in. Steam billows out before I close the door, locking myself in there with her.

"Asher?" Sydney's voice sounds slightly panicked as she says my name, her head ducking out past the shower curtain. I watch the relief flood her expression as she lets out a sigh. "You scared the shit out of me."

"Sorry, babe." I smirk, grabbing the back of my shirt as I pull it over my head. "You got room in there for me?"

A fire burns in Sydney's hooded gaze. "Always," she murmurs, licking her lips as she watches me undress.

Leaving my clothes on the floor, I walk over to the shower as she pulls open the curtain and I step inside with her. Sydney backs up, stepping back into the water as she gives me space to enter. Her body is wet and slick, glistening from the water. I follow along after her, stepping into her space as I wrap my arms around her waist.

Sydney pulls me into the water with her, the steam surrounding us as the hot spray spills down both of our bodies. "Perfect timing, showing up in time to get in here with me."

"Let me wash you," I murmur, releasing one arm from her waist as I reach over for her loofah. I squirt some of her bodywash into it. Taking a small step away from her, Sydney drops her arms to her sides as I bring the loofah to her chest and begin to work a lather with the soap. Her eyelids flutter shut as I scrub the front of her body.

Dropping to my knees in front of her, I scrub her legs. She stares down at me, a fire burning in her irises as I bring my face close to her pussy. I hear the sharp intake of her breath as I press my lips to hers, kissing her before I rise back up to my feet.

"Tease," Sydney growls at me, frowning in disapproval.

A smirk forms on my face as I slowly turn her around to have her back facing me. Leaning forward,

I nip at the lower lobe of her ear. "Patience, babe. I'll give you everything you want in a little bit."

"Fine," she groans, planting her hands on the wall in front of her as I lather her back with more soap. Using the loofah I scrub with one hand, while I use my other and massage her flesh. Sydney moans softly, her body relaxing under my touch.

"Come to Maine with me."

I don't bother easing into the conversation, because I know Sydney will shut me down immediately. She hates talking about the future because of the uncertainty of it all.

Dropping her hands from the wall, she spins around to face me. "What do you mean?"

"I mean that I don't want to spend a fucking second away from you, Sydney," I tell her, stepping closer as I cup the side of her face. "I want you to come spend the summer with me in Maine. I want you to spend the rest of your fucking life with me, but I'm not proposing yet because I want that shit to be perfect."

Sydney's eyes widen slightly, her lips parting slightly, as she stares back at me. She's silent for a moment, her throat bobbing as she swallows hard. "You want me to come with you?"

"Sydney," I murmur, dropping the loofah as I

cup both sides of her face. "When will you see how absolutely crazy I am about you? You're my endgame. I don't want anyone else in this lifetime but you." I pause for a moment, my eyes bouncing back and forth between hers. "I don't want you to feel pressured if you don't want to go, but I want you with me."

She continues to stare at me, like she's at a loss for words. "I don't want to live life without you and that scares the shit out of me, because I have no idea what the future holds, especially if you go to the NHL."

"The future holds us, Sydney."

"You want that with me?" she asks, her voice cracking around her words as she's overcome with emotion.

A smile pulls on the corners of my lips. "More than I've ever wanted anything else in my life."

Tears fill her eyes before they spill, mixing with the water that streams down the sides of her face. "I'll come to Maine with you. I'll follow you wherever you go, Asher."

"I won't be going anywhere without you, babe."

Sydney steps closer to me, wrapping her arms around my neck as my hands find her waist. I pull her flush against me, her naked body pressed to mine. "This isn't an official proposal, because I have plans for it already, but I can't wait any longer to ask you." I pause for a moment, swallowing over the lump in my throat. "I want you to have my last name and have my babies. Will you marry me, Sydney?"

Her eyes bounce back and forth between mine. "I would love nothing more than to be your wife." She lifts up on her tiptoes as I dip my face down to hers, our lips lightly brushing against each other's. "Yes, Asher Golding. I will marry you."

"Thank fuck," I breathe, nipping at her bottom lip. "I couldn't wait any longer to ask, but you'll get your ring with my official proposal."

"So, this is all just a tease?"

A laugh rumbles in my chest. "No, babe, just a taste of what's to come."

Pulling away from her, I begin to make my way down her naked body as I pepper kisses along every inch of skin. Dropping to my knees in front of her, I grab the back of her knee and hook her leg over my shoulder.

"Now, it's my turn to have a taste of what's to come…"

ASHER AND SYDNEY BONUS SCENE

Sydney lifts her gaze to mine as I roll over in bed to look at her. We're leaving in a few short hours for our honeymoon and it still seems unreal that our wedding day was yesterday. We had a small wedding in Maine, in my hometown, surrounded by our family and friends.

Since our relationship first started around Christmas, we decided to have a Christmas wedding. It was magical and no, I don't feel lame saying that. Sydney looked like a delicate snowflake, dressed in white, as she floated toward me at the altar.

We exchanged our vows before sliding our wedding rings over our fingers. Lifting my hand into the air, I look at the white gold band around my finger as a smile touches my lips.

"You're up early." She smiles at me, still naked from when we fell into bed together last night. "You okay?"

I nod, smiling at her. "Just reliving yesterday in my head. Thank you for making me the happiest man in the world."

"I love you, Asher," she breathes, stroking the sides of my face. "There's no one else I would want to spend the rest of my life with."

Scooting closer to her, I wrap her in my arms as I pull her body flush against mine. "Good, because you're stuck with me now, baby."

Sydney laughs lightly as I roll her onto her back, settling between her legs. My cock is already hard, as it usually is when she's naked and around me. "Well, good morning to you too," she chuckles as the tip presses against her center. She lifts her legs, wrapping them around my waist as I sink inside her. "Mmmm."

"Good morning, Mrs. Golding," I murmur, planting my lips along the side of her neck as I sink deep inside her. "My beautiful, amazing wife."

"Stop," she moans. "You're going to blow my head up if you keep talking like that."

"I'll never stop telling you the truth, baby," I whisper in her ear, dragging my tongue along the outer shell. "You can count on me to always inflate your ego."

Sydney's nails are in my back, leaving her mark on my skin as I begin to move my hips, thrusting in and out of her. It isn't our first time together, but every time feels even better than the last. And knowing she's now my wife adds a whole new dimension to us. I can't seem to ever get enough of Sydney.

"Don't stop," she moans as I begin to thrust harder into her.

"As you wish, my queen," I murmur against her neck as I move my hips. Each thrust is harder and we're both breathless as we inch closer to our climax. If I died right now, I would die the happiest man. Sydney is my entire world and I'll spend the rest of my days getting lost in her.

Her legs are around my waist, her pussy constricting around my cock as she gets closer to the edge. Rocking my hips, I hit all of the right places inside of her before she's free falling. I'm right behind her, losing myself inside her as I fill her with my cum. We ride on a cloud of euphoria together with not a single care in the world.

"I love you, Sydney," I tell her as I lift my head to meet her gaze.

"Forever and always, babe." She smiles up at me, her face overcome with ecstasy from her orgasm. "I love you."

I slowly slide out of her, settling on the bed beside her. Wrapping my arms around her, I pull her flush against my side as both of our hearts pound in tandem together. We should really be getting ready to leave for the airport, but that can wait.

Right now, I want to soak up this moment.

Loving my wife.

NEXT IN THE SERIES

Splintered Ice is the sixth book from the Wyncote Wolves, featuring Sterling and Olivia. It is a grumpy/sunshine, best friend's brother college hockey romance!

Continue reading on the next page for a look inside Splintered Ice.

PROLOGUE
STERLING

"Yo, Barrett," Simon calls after me as we head out of the locker room after practice. It's our first practice back together after winter break. A brand-new semester and we're gearing up for the most important games of our college career. "You wanna go grab some beers?"

Simon has been my roommate since junior year. We shared our house with Hayden when he first moved here, but since he and Eden became exclusive, he moved out. Simon and I decided to let Vaughn Carter move in with us. He's a freshman at Wyncote this year, but he is practically a goddamn prodigy.

The kid is destined for greatness and there are talks of him going pro before graduating college. I wish I were going to be around to see how things pan out for him, but the rest of us are all going to be graduating this year.

"Hell yeah," I tell him, nodding enthusiastically. "I'll meet you at O'Hallarans?"

"Sounds good," Simon agrees as he heads through the parking lot in the direction of his car. Sometimes we drive together to save on gas, but he had to run some errands after class so I didn't bother questioning him.

After throwing my hockey equipment into the trunk, I hop into the front seat of my car. As I turn on the engine, my phone connects to the car and it begins to ring. Glancing at the screen, a groan slips from my lips as I see my little sister's name flashing across the screen.

"What's up, Stella?" I answer, attempting to keep the irritation from my voice. She's three years younger than me and decided to move across the country to attend college. It pissed my parents off, but I was secretly thankful. Don't get me wrong, I love my little sister and will protect her with my life... but goddamn if she doesn't get on my nerves sometimes.

When I spoke to her two days ago, she was trying to get me to send her some money to go out since our parents wouldn't. They want her to get a job, since they're paying for her schooling. Being the brother that I am, I sent her some, but it feels like she only calls me when she needs something now.

"Hey, big brother!" Her voice is energetic and she sounds like she's bouncing off the walls. I know she's been partying and shit, but sometimes I wonder what she's really getting herself into. "Is now a bad time?"

"Nope, just finished practice and I'm heading to the bar."

"Okay, cool," she says, pausing for a moment. "So, I have a huge favor to ask of you."

Internally, I groan, closing my eyes for a second before pulling out onto the road. "What is it?" God knows what the hell she's going to be asking of me now.

"So... Olivia just transferred to Wyncote this semester."

My eyebrows pull together as I drive closer to the bar. "Olivia? Like your best friend since kindergarten?"

"Yes, stupid," Stella scoffs, and I swear I can hear her rolling her eyes. "As if there is any other Olivia who practically lived at our house."

I swallow hard, my mind drifting back to Olivia

Davis. I haven't seen her since I left for college. She was only fifteen at the time, still practically a child. She always wanted to be treated like she was older, but I couldn't bring myself to view her as anyone other than my little sister's best friend. I literally could not allow myself to look at her any other way.

"Why's she coming to Wyncote?"

"Well, she's majoring in biology. For some reason, Wyncote is supposed to have a better program for whatever it is she's doing." Stella pauses for a moment and I hear someone talking in the background but she shushes them. "I honestly don't remember why she said it was better there. Either way, she's there... like now."

"And this affects me, how?"

Stella sighs. "Can you not be an asshole for like two seconds?"

"Can you maybe call me sometime when you don't need something from me?"

Stella laughs. "Don't act like you would actually want to talk to me. Unless it has to do with hockey, you tend to tune everyone out."

My jaw tightens, but I don't bother arguing with her. As I pull my car into a spot in the parking lot at O'Hallarans, I see Simon as he walks inside. "Get to the point, Stella. I need to get off the phone."

"Olivia just moved there and doesn't know a single person. Can you do me a favor and just, like, check up on her? Maybe make sure she's okay and keep an eye out on her?"

"Don't you think she's old enough to take care of herself?" I question my sister as I turn off the engine of my car and switch the call back to my phone. Climbing out of the car, I hold it to my ear before slamming the door shut behind me.

Stella groans through the phone and I can tell she's getting frustrated with me. It's only natural; it's the relationship we have together. There was a point where we got along really well, until we both started to grow up and grow apart. I will always look out for her, but we are definitely in two different places in our lives right now.

"Please, Sterling," Stella practically begs. "You know I wouldn't ask something like this from you if it wasn't important to me."

A sigh slips from my lips as I make my way closer to the entrance of the bar. "Fine," I agree, not entirely pleased about the entire situation. "How the hell do you expect me to find her? I'm not going to go search the dorms looking for her. Do you know where she's living or anything about her being here."

"Look," my sister says, her words rushing out. "I'm gonna text you her number and just shoot her a message. Meet up with her and shit. I don't know, just let me know as soon as you do."

"What? No. I'm not going to do—"

"Thanks, Sterling!" Stella is rushing me off the phone now and her tone is filled with excitement. "I knew I could count on my big brother. You're seriously the best. Sending her number now, love you!"

Stella ends the call before I even get the chance to say anything to her in response. She completely set me up. I agreed to check in on her friend and keep an eye out on her, but I didn't need her damn number. If Stella could have just given me some information about her, I could have figured it out without having to meet up with her.

A text comes through from Stella with Olivia's number and a reminder to send her a message ASAP and then to let Stella know. Groaning, I save the number in my phone and open my messages. I stare at the screen for a moment as I linger outside the door of O'Hallarans, not knowing what the fuck to say.

STERLING

Hey, is this Olivia? This is Sterling, Stella's brother.

I cringe, rereading my message. What the hell even was that? The stupidest thing I've ever sent. Sighing, I lock my phone and put it into the front pocket of my hoodie before heading into the bar.

Simon is already sitting there waiting for me. He turns to face me, handing me a beer that he already ordered for me as I drop down onto the barstool next to him. "I talked to Greyson. He's heading over here then."

"Cool," I respond, nodding as I lift the beer to my lips and take a sip. My phone vibrates in my front pocket and I pull it out. I see Olivia's name on the screen and exhale deeply.

"Who's Olivia?" Simon questions me, his nosey ass looking over my shoulder at my phone.

Turning my head to him, I narrow my eyes, my lips pursed. "My little sister's best friend. She just moved here and Stella wanted me to check in on her."

"Ooh," Simon raises his eyebrows, "is she hot?"

I drive my shoulder into his, pushing him away. "Fuck off and don't even think about it."

Simon chuckles, turning his direction back to

the TV at the hockey replays as I open Olivia's message. My jaw tics as my eyes scan the screen.

OLIVIA

> Hi Sterling! How are you doing? I don't know if Stella told you, but I just moved to Wyncote.

She's just as fucking bubbly as I remember. And I hate it. That's how Olivia always was. The kindest, most caring person I had ever met. And she got under my skin like no other with the way positivity just rolled off her. She's like a ray of fucking sunshine and I would much rather see dark clouds lining the sky.

STERLING

> Stella did tell me. She wanted me to check in on you and make sure you were good.

Fuck what Stella wanted. I'm not meeting up with Olivia if I don't have to. If she doesn't need my help with anything, then there's no need.

OLIVIA

> I'm good! Just getting settled in and adjusting to life here :)

She would send a goddamn smiley face emoji. Grabbing my beer, I take another sip of it before sending my last response to her for the night.

STERLING

Cool. If you need anything, let me know.

I send a quick message to my sister, letting her know I talked to Olivia. Before either of them can respond, I put my phone on silent and lay it on the bar facedown. I'll do what my sister asked of me in terms of making sure Olivia is good.

We may have been close at one point, but that doesn't mean we were ever friends.

She's my sister's best friend, not mine.

ALSO BY CALI MELLE

<u>WYNCOTE WOLVES SERIES</u>

Cross Checked Hearts

Deflected Hearts

Playing Offsides

The Faceoff

The Goalie Who Stole Christmas

Splintered Ice

Coast to Coast

Off-Ice Collision

ABOUT THE AUTHOR

Cali Melle is a contemporary romance author who loves writing stories that will pull at your heart-strings. You can always expect her stories to come fully equipped with heartthrobs and a happy ending, along with some steamy scenes and some sports action. In her free time, Cali can usually be found spending time with her family or with her nose in a book. As a hockey and figure skating mom, you can probably find her freezing at a rink while watching her kids chase their dreams.